HOS... ...LE

INDIE PUBLISHER

ROSEL & FERRULE

INDIE PUBLISHER

THE TRACKS WE MAKE

MICHAEL McGRUTHER

For the Rust Belt Dreamers

Life is a long journey home, where we begin is often where we return. The tracks we make, tell our story.

GHOST TOWN

The moment I read the tragic Facebook post, a floodgate of memories burst open, each one a relic from the year that broke me, the year that drove me to flee and never look back. And yet, here I was, on the cusp of a reluctant homecoming, my car idling on the shoulder of the highway, only a mile from the exit that led directly to my past.

My hands gripped the wheel, knuckles white, as if I could hold onto the present a little longer. From this vantage point, Snydersville looked almost idyllic, like a scene from a storybook. Smoke spiraled from distant chimneys, framing rustic farms and weathered silos.

It was a picturesque lie, a facade concealing something darker that I knew all too well.

I stared into the valley, lost in reflection, when a silver Greyhound bus roared past too close, shaking my car in its wake. I watched it shift gears and take the exit ramp about a mile down the road, its form shrinking until it vanished from sight, pulling my imagination along with it.

Spring of 1991. That's where my mind settled. I was a senior at Snydersville High, a kid barely scraping by academically, pitied more than respected, growing up on the wrong side of the tracks where dreams and factories both died.

I was one of the lucky ones, or so I thought. But life has a way of pulling you back, forcing you to confront the ghosts you thought you'd left behind.

1991

My senior year was a masterclass in the art of survival. Mornings were a tactical operation, executed with military precision. The objective? Get out of the house before my alcoholic older brother Troy woke up.

I'd been fending for myself since I was old enough to work, stretching every hard earned dollar until it screamed for mercy. My grooming routine was a lesson in minimalism: one bar of soap for everything until it disintegrated into nothingness. Then, it was time to scrape soap residue from the tray until I could pilfer another bar from the school's janitorial supplies. Survival often meant making choices that didn't exactly make me proud.

I had claimed our parents' old room, complete with a tiny, attached bathroom. It was the only sanctuary in a house that had seen better days. Once a home filled with the laughter and energy of a young family, it had deteriorated into a maze of clutter, chaos and memory land mines too painful to bring up.

Skipping breakfast was standard operating procedure. I'd tiptoe through the house, avoiding the evidence of Troy's sad existence—piles of records, cassette tapes, clothes, overflowing ash trays and boxes of God-knows-what. Occasionally, I'd have to sidestep a stranger, usually a woman in various stages of undress, a leftover from Troy's sad social life. The sight was always jarring, especially in the harsh light of morning.

Today, Troy was sprawled on the living room couch, a casualty of his own excesses. An empty whiskey bottle teetered on the armrest behind his head. He adjusted himself, tipping it over. It crashed to the floor as I passed. I froze. If he woke, he'd pick a fight with me over anything. I reached for the door, my fingers deftly manipulating the loose handle to avoid any creaks. Holding my breath, I stepped out into the new day, the door closing softly behind me. Another morning mission accomplished.

My bike lay flat on the front porch, hidden from prying eyes. Not that anyone would dare steal from our house; it was the one place people avoided like the plague. With its darkened windows and a front yard that looked more like a junkyard than a garden, our home was the last home at the end of our road.

I wrestled the bike down the uneven stairs and mounted it, backpack securely on.

Our house was perched atop Dobes Hill, offering a panoramic view of the riverbank, the old railroad car factory, and the downtown area beyond. My one daily dose of serenity came during the morning descent, when I could coast down the hill and take in the sunrise. That year, spring was fashionably late, but the morning sun still managed to cast a glow over the red factory buildings, transforming the mundane into something almost magical. These fleeting moments of beauty were my lifeline, but my bike? It was my oxygen.

Hitting the flatlands, I'd pray for a green light. If luck was on my side, I'd sail smoothly into town, barely pedaling. "Work smart, not hard," my dad used to say.

The route to school was a grim tour of all the bars where Troy squandered his nights—and his life. Each one had a name more ironic than the last, but Troy's go-to, where he spent almost all of his time, was Big Lucky's. The truth wasn't lost on me, even back then. He was anything but lucky, drowning sorrows that he only compounded with each drink. I despised those bars and the self-loathing they harbored as if it was a virtue to be drunk. Maybe that's why I never touched alcohol besides a few times, and still don't. It's as if I knew, even as a kid, that those places were quicksand in the valley, and once you're in, it's almost impossible to get out.

After the bars, I rolled through the downtown strip, a shadow of its former self. Most storefronts were vacant, save for a few holdouts—a donut shop popular with aging veterans, the Pizza King, the bank, and the Texas Hots Cafe. It was the arrival of Walmart a few years back that had been the first death knell for local businesses. By the time I hit ninth grade, downtown had already started its rapid decline, and it hadn't recovered since.

Veering off Main Street, my eyes darted to the bank clock. I had minutes to spare. Tardiness was a recurring issue for me, a habit I couldn't seem to shake. I pedaled like mad, crossing a bridge and descending the other side at breakneck speed. Swinging a sharp left onto school grounds, I pulled up to the rack outside the front doors and chained my bike, hoping I'd go unnoticed. But as I snapped my lock into place, the final bell rang, sealing my fate. I was late again.

I walked towards the front door with my head down and my backpack slung over my shoulder. Principal Day was standing on the other side of the entrance waiting with his arms crossed and a look of disappointment that I saw a lot in those days.

"Tardy again, Pete. I thought we discussed this?"

I hesitated, "We did, but-"

He interrupted, cutting me off and grabbing me by the shoulder, "But what? You need to be punctual in life. This is the last few weeks of your senior year. Come June you'll get to walk out of those doors with a diploma and a chance at life. Isn't that what you want?"

"A chance at life? That is what I want."

"You need a diploma for that. Now get to class and don't let me catch you coming through those doors late tomorrow, Pete."

"Tomorrow's Saturday, Mr. Day," I said with a grin, walking past him and down the long hallway to my homeroom.

Principal Day was also the football coach and he treated everyone like they had potential if they could stick to the plan — his plan. The problem was, not everyone can stick to the plan because not everyone was made for that plan.

I spun the combination lock on my locker to drop off my bag. The words "scumbag" were scribbled in pencil across the metal door. It was nothing new; I'd been the target of such petty insults for years. With a well-practiced indifference, I used my sleeve to wipe away the words and headed into class as the Pledge of Allegiance concluded. I took my usual seat in the back corner near the window.

Mr. Logan peered at me over his glasses. "Tardy, Pete. That's strike two this week."

"Yep," I replied, settling into my chair.

Economics class had a predictable rhythm. Mr. Logan would sit quietly at his desk, engrossed in some document or book, taking his time before launching into the day's lesson. We'd all learned the hard way to keep quiet during this period. Mr. Logan had a short fuse and a meticulously planned agenda that he didn't appreciate being disrupted. Crossing him meant earning the title of "Mister," a surefire sign you were about to be sent to the main office for a stern talking-to. I'd had my share of those encounters over the years, but those days were mostly behind me. With only a fraction of my final quarter left, I couldn't afford to jeopardize my chances of graduating. That diploma, as I have been told since 9th grade, was my ticket to something better, and I wasn't about to let anything stand in my way.

I could feel Chad Parks' gaze boring into me from across the room. I looked over at him as he was busy molding a spit wad, using a hollowed-out pen as his weapon of choice. He mouthed, "You wanna die, scumbag?" I averted my eyes; this was merely another day in the life of being Chad's target. He had it out for me since 4th grade, and sported the same buzz cut since kindergarten with a perpetual sneer that looked permanently etched onto his ugly face. How he was popular, I couldn't understand, but he was. His side-kick, Will Cleveland, leaned into whisper something to him. A moment later, a wet slap hit the side of my neck. I turned to see Chad's smug grin.

"Take a look outside, McCloskey," he whispered.

I glanced out the window to my left and felt my stomach drop. A chain gang clad in orange jumpsuits picked up litter along the highway, supervised by guards from nearby Mapleton Correctional Facility. Another spit wad hit me.

"Knock it off with the spit-wads, Chad!"

With everyone now looking at me, Chad gestured toward the window. "Hey, check out the lifers. Bet some of 'em are killers. Right, McCloskey? You'd know a killer when you see one, wouldn't you? Point out which one's your daddy."

The room went quiet, then filled with nervous hushed laughter. Even Mr. Logan looked out the window. I kept my head down, my heart pounding. I had seen my father among the prisoners, but I couldn't bring myself to acknowledge it.

"Yep, that's McCloskey the killer," Chad jeered, eliciting another round of uncomfortable laughter from the class.

"Enough, Mr. Parks. Both you and Mr. McCloskey are going to the front office," Mr. Logan interjected.

"What did I do? I just want everyone to be safe," Chad retorted.

"You know exactly what you've done. Disrupting my class is unacceptable, whether it's day one or day one hundred and one," Mr. Logan said, walking over to pull down the window shades.

As the shades descended, I caught a final glimpse of my father, his broad shoulders hunched over, garbage bag in hand, glancing toward the school. I sank lower into my seat, wishing I could vanish into the floorboards. The weight of my family's dark history pressed down on me, heavier than ever in that moment.

• • •

P rincipal Day was meeting with another student when Mr. Logan escorted Chad and me into the main office. His face flushed red when he saw me, but I knew I wasn't the one at fault.

My friend Ricky Larson was already there, serving his second week of in-school suspension. He was facing the wall, his eyes directed at a poster about good hygiene. As I walked by, I gave Ricky a quick tap on the shoulder and took a seat next to the partially open door of Principal Day's office.

Inside, I heard him talking to Morgan Downer, the most unusual and downright beautiful girl in our class. She wasn't in trouble like the rest of us; she was already accepted to a big time university and was treated more like a student teacher than a student by the staff. She had a thick stack of papers in her hands.

"These are all checked and sorted. I'm helping out in Mrs. Wilkins' class later, for extra credit. Do you need anything else done around here?" Morgan said. I could see half of her face through the door, she was so beautiful to me that I didn't realize I was staring.

"Like you'd ever have a chance, McCloskey," said Chad.

Ricky looked over at me, his shoulders asking the unspoken question: What happened? I shook my head and subtly gestured toward Chad.

"I could kick both your asses at the same time if I wanted to," Chad boasted, puffing out his chest.

"Oh yeah? Why don't you try it right here, big guy?" Ricky retorted, his thick glasses giving him an air of unpredictability, which wasn't far from the truth when he was off his meds.

"Yeah, right, tough man," Chad sneered.

"That's enough out there, Ricky, or you'll get another hour of after-school detention in addition to in-school suspension," Principal Day warned, his voice carrying through the ajar door.

Ricky looked confused, but Chad straightened up as Morgan walked by. He pretended to slap her on the butt. I shot him a glare. Everyone thought Morgan was hot, but Chad stood no chance despite being the captain of the football team, and neither did anyone else. Morgan was a class apart, seemingly from another era. She kept to herself and didn't fit in with our rough crowd or hang out much. She was a loner like me as far as I could tell, no big circle of friends.

Principal Day stood in the doorway eyeing us. He had a soft spot for Chad because he was the star player on the school's football team, and everyone knew that no matter what Chad did, he wouldn't face severe consequences. He's the reason Snydersville won championships, and that gave him a sort of immunity that the rest of us could only dream of, even now when school is coming to an end. It was a bitter pill to swallow, but it was another harsh reality of life in Sny High.

"Get in here Larson," said Principal Day.

I kept my head down. When Ricky's torn up Converse all-stars passed me I whispered "good luck, man."

Ricky pulled the door half closed behind him and sat down across from Day, who brandished a folder.

"Do you know what I have here?" said Principal Day while waving it in front of Ricky.

"Would that be my permanent record?"

"Correct. Your permanent record. And from the looks of it, your future's not looking too good and you might not even graduate."

Principal Day ran his finger across the top sheet and read out loud.

"Absent more than you've been here all year. Failing in every class except...home economics-"

"Fag," coughed Chad into closed hands but I didn't laugh. Principal Day stopped talking, leaned back and looked in our direction through the door.

"One hour after school detention, McCloskey."

"C'mon I didn't say anything, and I have work," I pleaded.

"Want another hour tomorrow? Keep talking."

After a long stare, he turned and looked at Ricky again.

"You're stuck with in-school suspension for acting up in class at least three times a week. Do you enjoy sitting and facing the wall doing assignments instead of learning in a classroom with everyone else?"

"It's not all bad, Mr. Day. I've learned it's better to keep clean and practice good hygiene or other kids might not wanna be my friends. Wish I knew this sooner to be honest," said Ricky, dead serious.

"I'm trying to level with you here, son. Have you been looking into vocational schools? Something in welding? Small fellas like yourself make decent welders."

Ricky lowered his head and clasped his hands together. He was always dramatic when he got in trouble. Ricky was the king of not caring what anyone thought and that's what I liked about him.

"I'm real sorry Mr. Day. My life at home is stressful. With a wife and two kids to feed I can't find time to behave in school. This is where I come to blow off steam and relax, ya know?" said Ricky in his textbook seriousness that is impossible to tell if he's joking. Principal Day looked down at him.

"Alright Ricky. Have it your way. Keep thinking the whole world is a big stupid joke. Wait and see what that attitude gets you. A bunch of nothing, that's what. Get out of my office and get back to the suspension seat. You can stay there until the very last day of school. I'm through trying to help you."

Ricky walked past me with his head down and a big grin. He loved messing with Principal Day, and he did not care about his grades one bit.

"Parks, McCloskey — get in here." his eyes narrowing on me as he beckoned for us to enter his office. The room smelled of stale coffee and old books, a testament to the years Principal Day had spent behind that desk. He was a large man, his physique a relic from his own football days, and he had a way of filling the room that went beyond his physical presence.

"Sit down, both of you," he commanded, pointing to the two chairs opposite his desk. We obeyed, Chad smirking as he took his seat.

"I've had enough of this perpetual nonsense and bullying," Principal Day began, his eyes darting between us. "You two have been at each other's throats for years, and I'm not tolerating it anymore. You're both on the cusp of adulthood, and let me tell you, the real world doesn't have time for this kind of petty squabbling."

He turned his attention to Chad. "You're heading to Elmira to play college football. Do you think they'll put up with this kind of behavior there? You're representing not only yourself but also this school and this town. Don't mess it up."

Chad nodded, his grin fading for a moment.

"And you, Pete," Principal Day continued, turning to me. "You've got your own path to figure out. You don't need this kind of distraction that's followed you around for years. You both need to leave the past in the past and move on into your futures. Understand me?"

I opened my mouth to protest, to point out that it was always Chad who instigated these confrontations, but Principal Day cut me off.

"I don't want to hear it. I don't care who started what or when. What I care about is that it ends, now. If it doesn't, I won't hesitate to take disciplinary action against either of you, even this close to graduation. Am I clear?"

We both nodded, the weight of his words settling over us. Chad had more to lose than me, but I wanted to be left alone.

"Now get out of my office and go back to class. And remember, the choices you make now will follow you for the rest of your lives."

As we left the office, Chad shot me a triumphant grin, as if he'd won some sort of victory. It was the same grin he always wore when he knew he'd gotten the better of me. But as I walked away, I couldn't help but think about Principal Day's words. We were on the cusp of adulthood, and the real world was waiting. It was time to leave the past behind. Whether Chad was ready to or not, it's all that I ever wanted — to not be haunted by the past.

REMEDIAL MATH

I stared at the math problem before me, my mind going blank. Numbers had always been my Achilles' heel, a jumble of figures that refused to make sense. I pretended to work, doodling aimlessly in the margins of my workbook, hoping to avoid drawing attention to myself.

Remedial math took place in a small room with no windows. It was once a janitor's storage closet, but now it held four desks evenly spaced and one teacher's desk facing them. The walls were white painted brick, making everything come into extreme focus. The room felt even smaller than usual; its claustrophobic dimensions intensified by Morgan's unexpected presence at the teacher's desk since she was already working on college credits.

She sat there, poised and confident like a teacher, as she graded papers in our teacher's absence. The air felt thick, and the neon lights above buzzed louder than usual, casting a harsh glare. I glanced at my workbook, its pages filled with juvenile illustrations about sharing apples, and felt a pang of embarrassment because I had always been drawn to Morgan, but I couldn't quite put my finger on why. Maybe it was her intelligence, her grace, or the way she seemed to exist in a different universe than the rest of us. Today, that universe had collided with mine, and I was painfully aware of and embarrassed by my own inadequacies in this subject. I didn't want her to know how dumb I was.

Morgan rose from her desk and began to circulate around the room, her eyes scanning our workbooks as she passed. My heart raced as she approached me, her perfume filling the air, a scent that smelled as sophisticated as she was. I angled my workbook away, attempting to shield my ineptitude from her gaze.

"Do you need some help with that last problem, Pete?" she asked, leaning over my desk, her hair cascading down like a waterfall and a touching my shoulder a bit.

"Um...I... uh..." I stammered, my words failing me.

"When you divide the apples, there's not an even amount to share among the friends, so you have to sub-divide the remaining parts into fractions," she explained, her voice calm and measured.

"I did that, but I keep getting the wrong number of slices," I mumbled, my eyes avoiding hers.

"It looks like you're rushing through it. Take your time, visualize yourself sharing and you'll get the right answer," she advised.

Her words swirled around me, but they might as well have been in a foreign language. My eyes darted to the clock, then back to my doodles, anywhere but the very basic math problem that mocked me from the page. I felt trapped, cornered by my own limitations, and as much as I needed her help, I wanted nothing more than to be left alone in that moment.

The bell rang, its shrill tone cutting through the

tension like a knife. I snapped my workbook shut, almost knocking into Morgan as I did.

"I can help you finish it later if you'd like," she offered, her eyes meeting mine.

"No thanks, you're not my teacher," I retorted, my words tinged with a bitterness I hadn't intended and did not mean.

Morgan paused, her gaze steady and unfazed. "Alright, if you change your mind, I'm around," she said, turning back to the teacher's desk, effectively closing the conversation.

I lowered my head and hurried out of the room. As I stepped into the hallway, I couldn't shake the feeling that I had missed an opportunity, not just to understand fractions, but to connect with someone who existed in a world I could only dream of entering, someone I secretly admired for how normal she was and someone who was way out of my league.

The hallway buzzed with the chatter of senior voices filling the hallway as we made our way to lunch. I kept to the periphery like always, hugging the locker-lined walls as I descended the stairwell to the lower floor.

The cafeteria was already packed, the lunch line snaking its way back into the hall. I took my place at the end, pulling out my remedial math workbook. Morgan's advice echoed in my mind: visualize and focus. I scribbled down the correct answer, but as I did, someone bumped me from behind and my pencil slipped from my fingers and clattered to the floor. Before I could retrieve it, Chad's foot shot out, sending it skittering across the room.

"It's over there, McCloskey. Don't worry, I'll hold your spot for ya," Chad sneered.

I retrieved my pencil, its tip now broken. I

clenched it in my hand, my knuckles turning white as I returned to my spot in line. Chad stepped aside, but only because Principal Day was nearby, his arms crossed, surveying the cafeteria line like a hawk.

"You look like you're gonna stab someone with that, McCloskey," Will muttered, barely audible. "Must run in the family." He and Chad never tired of their own insults.

Ignoring them, I slid the broken pencil above my ear and out of the corner of my eye, I saw Morgan enter the cafeteria. She sat alone at a nearby table, unpacking her brown bag lunch with a posture that looked almost adult-like. She made a small sign of the cross before eating, her movements imbued with a simple dignity. She'd been this way for as long as I can remember.

The line moved, and I found myself face-to-face with Mrs. Jo, the lunch lady. Her face was a roadmap of hard living, her nose bearing the telltale signs of a life spent in the company of too much alcohol. It's a look you know when you see it around here.

"Pizza or taco salad?" she grunted.

"Taco salad," I replied, my voice barely above a whisper.

She heaped a generous portion of taco meat onto a bed of tortilla chips, her movements mechanical but efficient. "Cheese, tomato, avocado?"

"Yes, yes, and yes."

My tray now full, I moved to the end of the line and presented my free lunch card for stamping. Chad and Will checked out before me, their pockets jingling with loose change.

"Free lunch for freeloaders. You and your dad both get a free ride from the state," Chad taunted, his voice tinged with disdain.

I ignored him, my eyes fixed on the cafeteria room as I made my way to a vacant table near the windows. I sat down, my eyes drifting to the bike rack outside, and began to eat. The food was mediocre at best, but it was sustenance, a lifeline in a home where the gas had long since been shut off, no fridge, and the microwave sat broken and unused.

As I ate, my eyes caught sight of the state prison bus pulling into the school lot. A knot of anxiety formed in my stomach as looked over my shoulders then out to the prisoners being led onto the bus by armed guards, their work for the day complete. Among them was my father. He paused for a moment, his eyes meeting mine through the glass, before being prodded forward by the barrel of a guard's rifle.

When the bus pulled away, I exhaled, my body sagging with relief. The weight of my family's dark history hung over me like a cloud, a constant reminder of a past I couldn't escape. Would it ever lift? I couldn't say for sure, but as I sat there, staring out the window, I noticed Morgan looking at me from across the room. I quickly got up, returned my tray and left.

STILSON'S FOOD
AND BEV

I talked my way out of after school detention because Principal Day knew that I work after school up at Stilson's. He's one of our biggest customers. I got to work there on a technicality because there were some food items you could buy, but really it was a big liquor store that served a town with a large supply of functioning drunks and I knew who was and wasn't an alcoholic. Stilson paid me good and in cash because I was dependable and didn't ask questions.

The liquor store was a short bike ride into North Snydersville from school, up the county road near the outskirts of town. The parking lot was always busy this time of day and as much as I hated what booze did to Troy, it was the only clean and well-run place in town besides Walmart and a few downtown spots. If you didn't have a factory job, you worked at Walmart, a grocery store or were on disability or welfare. I was lucky to have the job that I did.

"Happy Friday, Pete," said Mr. Stilson, glad to see me arrive at work on time. Mr. Stilson was a dying breed in Snydersville, a kind and gentle soul who radiated with the warmth and wisdom of a bygone era. He'd retired from the postal service at the age of 40, trading in his mailbag for the keys to the liquor store he'd now owned for twenty years. I'd known him since I was a kid, back when he was our mailman during better times. That's how I got the job I had now. He'd always greet me with a smile, asking how school was going and if I'd been keeping out of trouble.

I remember one summer day when I was about ten, he let me tag along on his mail route for a little while because I wanted to be a mailman too. At the time, I thought it was the coolest thing ever, getting to ride shotgun in the mail truck, watching him expertly sort through letters and packages as he navigated the winding roads of our small town. Looking back, I realize it must've been somewhat annoying for him, having a curious kid asking a million questions while he was trying to focus on work. But he never showed it, answering each query with patience and good humor.

"See this, Pete?" he'd said, holding up a stack of letters. "Each one of these is a story, a connection between people. Never underestimate the power of a simple message shared between people."

That day stuck with me, and as I grew older, I came to appreciate Mr. Stilson for more than his kindness and compassion. He was a source of good advice that I didn't take as much advantage of as I should, always willing to lend an ear when I needed it. Whether it was family trouble, school stress, or any drama, he'd listen intently, nodding along before offering up some nugget of wisdom.

"Life's a series of ups and downs, Pete," he'd often say. "The key is to ride the highs and weather the lows, knowing that nothing lasts forever." And my other favorite, "Action and reaction are two words that make

the world go around. How you react will define everything that happens to you."

It was advice like this that made me value working
at Stilson's beyond the money he paid me. He knew
my story better than anyone and I was loyal because
of it.

"There was a spill in the cooler. I need that
cleaned up right away," he said.

I nodded, grabbing my apron from its hook in the
back room and tying it around my waist. The fabric
was stained from years of spills and mishaps, but it
was a part of the uniform, a badge of honor in a town
where opportunities were few and far between. I
picked up the broom and headed to the back left-hand
cooler, its glass doors fogged over from the constant
temperature changes.

Inside, the cooler was a mess. Spilled wine and
sticky residue coated the shelves, a testament to the
carelessness of inebriated customers. I rolled up my
sleeves as I grabbed a bucket of soapy water and a
scrub brush. It was a dirty job, but it was honest work,
and it paid in ways other than money.

Cleaning and organizing the cooler at Stilson's was
more than a menial task for me; it was a form of ther-
apy, a way to impose order on a world that often felt
chaotic and out of control. Each bottle I wiped down,
each shelf I rearranged, felt like a small victory against
the disorder that plagued my home and school life. I
couldn't control Troy's mess or the disarray that defined our existence, but here, in this cooler, I could
make things right, even if for a little while. The contrast was stark, almost painful. At home, every mis-
placed item, every stack of unsorted papers, felt like a
physical manifestation of the turmoil that clouded my
life. But here, each item had a place, each space was

accounted for. It was as if I was trying to mend something broken within me through the simple act of cleaning.

As I scrubbed, my mind wandered. The cooler was like a microcosm of Snydersville itself—messy, complicated, but somehow still functioning. I thought about the people who walked through these doors, each one a character in the ever-unfolding, yet never changing drama of small-town life. There were the regulars, their faces etched with the lines of hard living, and the weekend warriors, their eyes alight with the promise of temporary escape. And then there were people like Principal Day, respectable on the surface but nursing their own private struggles behind closed doors.

I wasn't always so detail-oriented, but in that cooler, my focus sharpened to a point that bordered on obsessive-compulsion. I found myself aligning the bottles to the millimeter, ensuring the labels faced forward, creating a sense of symmetry and balance. It was a small thing, but it gave me a sense of accomplishment, a feeling of control that was sorely lacking elsewhere.

"How's it going in there?" Mr. Stilson's voice broke through my reverie, pulling me back to the task at hand.

"Almost done," I called back, giving the shelves one final scrub before rinsing them down.

"Good. Once you're finished, restock the Bell Agio chianti. We've got a shipment in the back that needs to go out."

I nodded, making a mental note as I closed the cooler door, taking a final look at my handiwork, I felt a sense of peace, however fleeting. It was as if, in tidying up that small space, I'd managed to clean a corner of my soul, giving me the strength to face another day in a life that often felt like a never-ending cycle of sadness and then struggle.

The Bell Agio chianti was a popular item, especially among the older crowd who still clung to the notion that a good bottle of cheap wine could elevate even the most mundane of evenings.

As the night wore on, the flow of customers increased, most of them already showing signs of inebriation as they stumbled in fooling nobody. The way they carried their beer out, clutching it like a lifeline, always struck me funny. They'd walk in with a sense of urgency, as if chasing some elusive dragon that promised to numb their pain, and then leave cradling their purchase as if it were a rescued animal to be taken home and nursed. Their faces were always a bit brighter on the way out, a temporary relief from whatever burden they carried in.

Watching them, I couldn't help but think about the different ways we all seek to restore some semblance of order or happiness in our lives. For them, it was the promise of escape in a bottle; for me, it was the satisfaction of turning a disordered space into something clean and organized, a cope I could not access at home.

I headed to the back, locating the new wine cases and hauled them out to the sales floor. As I stocked the shelves, surrounded by bottles that promised a world of sophistication, the irony was our town had long since lost its luster. For too many, the only way to pretend it didn't happen was to drink until everything looked golden again. That was the thing about Snydersville I didn't understand back then. It was a town of contradictions, a place where dreams and reality coexisted in uneasy harmony, with reality winning most of the time. I realized that I was a part of it too, a character in this ever-darkening region, hit hard by changing economic times beyond anyone's control.

Mr. Stilson called me to the register and slipped a small brown envelope into my apron pocket, it was pay day. At home, I kept all of my savings well hidden, because my fear was that Troy would find my cash and drink it all away.

"I'm going run home to dinner a little early today because one of my granddaughters is visiting. Think you can handle the last hour alone?" said Stilson.

"No problem. You trained me well."

"Remember to lock all three front locks and make sure the back is locked too."

"You got it, Mr. Stilson."

"And put the money in the safe."

"First thing I always do."

"You're a good kid, Pete. I appreciate what you do for me here."

He grabbed his keys, crossword puzzle, and book from the register counter and slipped out the back door. Even though I sucked at math, working at Stilson's was easy thanks to the computerized cash register that he had put in.

When he pulled out and waved goodbye one last time through the front window, I switched over the in-store music from country to the rock station. Def Leppard's Photograph started and I cranked it up, feeling cool and empowered in that last hour. If anyone asked where Stilson was, I always told them he was in the bathroom or back office, and I was minding the store for a minute. There wasn't a real risk of being robbed at gunpoint or anything like that because around here everyone knows everyone for the most part. Strangers never pass through town unnoticed and without a heavy dose of suspicion put upon them because Snydersville had an unspoken language of confrontation if you were not from around here and everyone knew it. To come to town and get drunk was fine, to come to town looking for a fight meant someone was getting beat up pretty bad — usually an out of towner who decided to talk crap. They all learn that when push comes to shove, town folk side with town folk.

I started closing up when the door jingled, and in walked two big guys whose faces looked vaguely familiar, like I'd seen them in the crowd at some high school game years ago. They were about Troy's age, and I wondered if they'd played against him back when times were better, back when he was someone else. They knew exactly who I was.

"Hey, kid, where's your loser brother?" The one who spoke had a build that reminded me of a grown-up Chad Parks, but with a mullet and beady eyes set too close together.

"I couldn't tell you. I'm not his keeper. Maybe try Lucky's?" I replied.

"Tell him to stay the hell away from Amanda. She's done with him."

"Trust me, he doesn't listen to me."

"He better, if he knows what's good for him."

"And who should I say is giving him this friendly advice?"

"Oh, he knows who I am."

"I don't," I retorted, but before I could say anything more, he lunged forward, grabbing me by the collar. The stench of alcohol filled the air between us.

"Randall, cut the shit. Not here, you idiot," his friend intervened, pulling him off me, then taking a can of Skoal from the counter display and smacking it with his pointer finger as he shook the can with one hand. He opened it and placed a fresh wad of chaw in his mouth, placing it in his cheek.

"You gotta pay for that. One fifty," I said. He handed me two dollars, and I gave him back thirty pennies and two dimes.

"Sorry, I'm short on quarters."

He pocketed the dimes, leaving the pennies on the counter. "Keep the change."

Randall, not missing a beat, swiped his hand across the counter, sending the pennies scattering across the floor. "Clean it up," he sneered while walking out like he was on a mission.

"Hey, don't come back!" I shouted as they exited. I moved to the door and watched them climb into an old green Ford pickup truck. The strains of Zeppelin's "I'm all outta love" filled the air as they peeled out of the parking lot, leaving a cloud of dust illuminated by the red neon glow of the store's sign.

I locked the locks, closed up, counted the money, locked it in the safe, turned down the lights and pulled my bike out through the back door. The night sky was clear, stars twinkling like distant dreams, too far to be grabbed, but always within view. I pedaled home at a leisurely pace, hoping to avoid crossing paths with Troy during his nocturnal bar crawl but also wondering what they meant about Amanda, who was Troy's ex-high-school sweetheart. I hadn't seen her around in years.

Navigating my way through the tree-lined side streets of Snydersville, I was keenly aware of the weekend rituals that unfolded around me. The town had its own secret spots where high schoolers would gather to drink away their teenage angst. Places like "the gravel pits," a barren stretch of land where bonfires would light up the night, and "the swimming hole," a secluded area near the river where the bravest —or drunkest—would take midnight dives. These were the domains where Chad reigned supreme, holding court like some kind of twisted school king. I was never invited to any of that, not that I would go. I knew I'd be nothing more than a target in Chad's obsession with wanting to kick my ass all the time.

The night air was thick with the smell of burning firewood. It was as if the whole town had conspired to create these pockets of drinking parties, these sanctuaries of bad decisions. And when the beer ran out, the party would descend from their hideaways in the hills, flooding Main Street with their rowdiness, looking for the next thrill, the next fight. Not a weekend passed without someone getting beat up for something. So, I took a detour, avoiding the main drag and the popular hangout spots. My tires hummed on the asphalt as I approached the short underground tunnel that passed beneath the train tracks, separating one side of Snydersville from the other. The lights flickered, making the graffiti painted on the tile walls come alive. Phrases like "Eat more pussy" and "Tanya sucks a mean one," sprinkled with racist scribbles, plus heavy metal band logos, and an abundance of love memorials by couples who came down here and made out before the cameras were installed.

I popped out of the other side and passed the VFW, avoiding the bars as I took the long way to the bottom of Dobes Hill where our house was.

When I got home the living room lights were still on. I snuck up onto the porch and lay my bike down. When I walked in Troy was sitting on the leather couch drinking a beer, waiting for me as I tried to run upstairs into my room when a crumpled can flew past my face.

"Get in here ya little fag."

"Don't call me that."

"Until I see a girl with you, you're a little fag."

"What do you want from me?"

"Rent's going up."

"You can't do that."

"Two fifty a month now. Yes, I can."

"I'm not even supposed to pay you nothin'. You cash the state checks that are supposed to be mine too."

He pounded the beer, crumpled the can with one hand and whipped it at my head again. I smacked it out of the air like an annoying bug.

"Two fifty," He said followed by a long gross burp. He stood up and combed back his hair while looking in a cracked living mirror and riffing on an invisible air guitar.

"And if you don't pay, you don't stay."

I knew he technically couldn't kick me out, but I also knew that he didn't care about what the rules were. Troy did not give one crap about anything but himself.

"Two big dudes came into Stilson's looking for you today. Said they were gonna kick your ass if you keep bothering Amanda."

Troy's eyes narrowed. "Who? That faggot Randall Fitz? That fuck thinks he can kick my ass? Tell him to come right over and knock on the door next time. I'll take him out like the fuckin' trash."

Troy cracked both knuckles and rotated his neck. He was pissed now but not at me. Knowing and that could change at any moment when he was drinking, I turned around to escape to my room, but he stopped me by grabbing my shoulder.

"I said rent is going up. Hand it over."

"No. Fuck you, Troy. Go get a job." I broke away and took off across the living room and into the back of the house. Troy chased after me, knocking over the kitchen table as he slid across the top and tackled me before I made it out the back door. Today's pay from Mr. Stilson was tucked into my pants, he tugged and searched my back pockets then flipped me over and held me with both hands.

"Where the fuck is it?!"

"It's not your money! I worked for it!"

"You owe me rent, faggot!"

"Stop calling me that!" I got my arms loose and snuck an uppercut through that landed on his chin and knocked him back. By the time he got up I was up too and ready this time. He nailed me in the center of the chest and knocked the wind out of me. I felt him digging the envelope out of my pants and taking the cash. By the time I got up he was long gone, slamming the living room door behind him.

"Fuuuuck you Troy!"

I made my way upstairs and took a fast cold shower and went to bed knowing I got mugged in my own house. It's a good thing I kept all of my savings off property, or I'd have nothing. I knew how Troy operated. He got our SSI checks, cashed them both and drank it all away. By the time the end of the month rolled around he'd be broke and start hitting me up for more drinking money. I felt sorry for him, but I couldn't let him keep robbing me like that. I lay there imagining what a typical Troy night out was like with my money in his pocket. He'd stroll down the hill to the bars, on a mission. He'd start out sitting at the Lucky's bar, drinking pints and talking shit while the games ended. By nine the places were all packed and Troy would usually be holding court out in the back area. When he got drunk, he was always charming and funny at first. I'd seen it so many times back when he was still in high school, the way he'd have everyone wrapped around his fingers, laughing at his impersonations and one-liners. Troy was Mr. Popular and class president a couple of years before I was a scumbag that nobody liked or talked to. I don't know what Troy could have been in life, but I do know all that time spent performing drunk was wasted time and wasted talent and I wasn't going to make the same mistakes if I could help it.

What I really needed was some parental guidance in life and there's only one place where I can find that.

BIG CREEK HILL

Daylight had a way of creating a sharp contrast to the dimness of my top floor room, a reminder that the world outside was waking up, even if I wasn't ready to. I skipped the shower, opting for a quick teeth-brushing and a splash of water through my hair. I was going for a long ride and would need another shower when I get home anyway. Slipping into my hoodie and jeans, I tiptoed down the creaky stairs, avoiding the spots I knew would give me away.

Riding a bike in Snydersville on an early Saturday morning was to be in a place suspended in time. It was as if everyone had collectively decided to sleep in, leaving the streets empty except for the occasional rust-bucket car badly in need of a muffler. As I pedaled through downtown, I noticed a Greyhound bus pulling up in front of Joe's Barber Shop. I hit the brakes and watched from across the street, intrigued. The display read "New York City," a place that sounded as distant as another planet from here.

The bus doors hissed open, and the driver's voice echoed, "Snydersville!" It was an invitation to get off here, but nobody did. Nobody got on either. The driver, a stocky black man with a beard, locked eyes with me for a moment as he pulled the lever that closed the doors and maneuvered the steering wheel, as massive as a boat's wheel. The bus roared back to life, leaving behind a cloud of exhaust that made me cough.

I got away from it, passed the school, my daily dread, and continued up the long road that led to the outskirts of town. When I reached Stilson's intersection, I took a right onto a county route and pushed myself to conquer Big Creek Hill. It was a challenging climb, exhausting to be honest, but the view from the top was so worth it.

I paused to catch my breath, my eyes drifting across the valley to Mapleton State Correctional Facility, perched on a distant hillside. Birds glided lazily in the sky, their freedom a stark contrast to that of the inmates within.

With a deep breath, I mounted my bike again and descended the other side of the hill. The wind in my face felt like a brief taste of freedom, a little escape from the gravitational pull of Snydersville. But as I coasted down, I couldn't shake the image of that empty bus, its open doors an unspoken question, a what-if that lingered in the air long after the exhaust fumes had dispersed.

It was a straight road on this side, and it gave me a bit of speed. Once I leveled out, I took both hands off the handle bar and coasted with the wind in my hair and my arms at my sides. It was always a relief to get outside of Snydersville even though where I was heading was not the happiest place in the world.

Mapleton was a lot smaller than Snydersville and the prison was where most of the people worked. Snydersville felt like a prison, but Mapleton was in fact a prison town. I rode my bike down from the winding country road to the prison entrance I knew too well. It was always imposing to approach its guard towers and castle-like walls. Barbed wire fence was so tall that I couldn't imagine anyone getting out but every once in a while, someone did. The guard at the entrance recognized me and waved me right through. I'm the only teen who comes here alone on a bicycle and they all know me now. I still had to get patted down after going through a metal detector, but the guards were all nice and I always did what they said.

A new prison guard led me to the visitation room. We passed a whole row of small visitation rooms where I would sometimes catch glimpses of the prisoner and their guest crying together. I always could feel the vibes around me and when sadness was thick, I had a deep reaction to it that I never enjoyed, like it landed on me too. The visitation wing emanated a tense sadness most of the time. If longing were a vibration, you felt it passing the rooms. Working here had to be depressing, but not as depressing as being locked up.

The guard led me to the designated room, his keys jangling as he unlocked the door. Inside, my dad, Billy McCloskey, sat behind the glass divider, dressed in an orange prison jumpsuit. Even confined and behind glass, he had a presence that filled the room. He looked up and smiled at me.

"One hour," the guard said, his voice devoid of emotion.

"Thank you. I know the drill," I replied.

The door closed behind me with a click, a sound that always made me feel like I was the one locked up.

I took a seat across from my dad, our eyes meeting through the glass.

"Hi, Dad."

"Son. You've grown at least two inches since the last time I saw you up close."

"I have? I barely eat."

"Why's that?"

"No time, really. I eat when I can."

"How was the ride over the hill today?"

"Pretty good. Spring's finally here. It's warming up."

"That's good to hear. I get some yard time after this because I've been on my best behavior. Tell me, Pete, what about Troy? Why doesn't that boy ever come up here with you?"

Dad's shoulders slumped, his eyes dropping to the table, pained by the hatred that Troy has for him, and himself.

"He's not doing well, Dad. It's hard living with him, real hard. He lost his license and is too lazy to bike this far. Plus, your car got impounded, and I'm not paying to get it out."

The weight of my words hung in the air. I could see the disappointment etched on his face, a reflection of the same pain he'd felt for years, but magnified by his inability to change anything from behind bars. Out in the world, he was a man of instant action. In there, he was kept from that part of himself. I know it hurt him, because I could read his body language.

"He's stealing from me, Dad. Even raised the rent on me like I'm made out of money."

"That little son of bitch is charging you rent. To live in my house?"

"He's hard up and I'm trying to make it through high school, so I can get away from him. I graduate, maybe, in a month and a half."

Dad sighed, his eyes meeting mine again. "I'm sorry I can't whoop Troy's ass into shape, son. But at least you have a job. That's more than many can say these days. I read the papers; I know it's getting tough out there and times are changing."

"I actually like working at Stilson's too. He's a good guy, gives me a lot of freedom. I make enough to get by and the customers are always interesting."

Dad's eyes softened, but I caught a flicker of something else—jealousy, maybe even bitterness. "You're lucky, Pete. Freedom is everything, and you have it."

"I know, Dad. That's why I'm planning to take more days off this summer to visit you. Our talks help me, and once high school's over, I'd like to see you more."

His eyes lit up, but the emotion was hard to read—a mix of joy and a kind of sorrow I couldn't quite place. "That's probably the best news I could get, Pete. It is lonely in here, but seeing your face, hearing about your life—it makes things a bit easier for me, even if it's a life I can't be a part of like I should."

"I know, Dad. Mr. Stilson said he'd think about it and let me know soon."

He sat back, crossed his arms and looked at me square. "You can tell old Stilson that after all the money I dumped into his place when he first got it, the least he can do is give me more time to visit with my son over the summer. Should be paid time if you ask me."

He smiled at me for a moment as if he was looking at himself in the past. I felt that pressure to live up to his expectations by not getting into trouble or being a failure like Troy. I wanted to make my dad proud. Between him and Troy I had two living examples of what not to do, but my father was my hero. He may have been locked away, but he didn't run away like my mother did and that's all that mattered to me.

"So. How's the girlfriend situation?" he said.

"The usual. I don't get noticed much." I slumped my head down, embarrassed that I was considered a scumbag and knew that no girls were interested in a guy like me for that reason. At least not the girl I was most attracted to.

"That's what we need to work on, then. Maybe you need to clean yourself up a little. I mean, look at you. You're a mess. If I were still at home, you'd never get out the front door looking like that. Why don't you splurge on some new clothes and a haircut down at the barber shop? Learn to take care of yourself like a man first and foremost. Then you'll start drawing the looks of the ladies."

I looked down at my faded and dirty jeans, worn out hoodie and crummy off-brand sneakers that only looked like Nikes when my pant legs were over half the shoe. I stopped trying to blend in with the popular kids years ago because I was a fraud and knew it.

"New clothes are expensive. And even if I did have stylish clothes there's not that many pretty girls in Snydersville at all," I deflected.

He looked at me and smirked.

Most kids have this kind of conversation with their father on the back porch in the summer or while out fishing, but for me it happened here in this visitation room with its bright lights and dark reality. Being raised by a prisoner felt staged because we were being watched by the guards.

"Pete, I ain't been in here all my life you know. There are always more than a few good-looking gals in every town across America. That's a fact. But you gotta

have a little self-respect before anyone is gonna respect you back. Know what I'm saying?"

"I got it. And yeah, maybe there's the one girl in
town I like but it's not like I'd ever have a chance with
her. It's not like I have tons of options."

"Look at me Pete. I am a man with no options. You
have plenty. Please don't ever forget that."

I was leaning in my chair again while he talked
more about how life was a series of small moments
strung together and my job was to make the most of
them one at a time. He reminded me that his decision
to make the worst out of one moment is what landed
him in here. One fateful moment and all he had to do
was react differently. Then he stopped talking and
looked at me differently, like he was noticing something about me for the first time.

"Straighten up," he said. "Don't slouch like that,
Pete. It's a sign of a weak individual. Someone who's
trying to hide from the world around him and be un-
seen. Someone who will never be man enough to win
over a real woman someday."

"Sorry, Dad. Nobody teaches me this stuff at all, ya
know?" I sat up, tall and straight.

"I understand. And I know you don't come all the
way over here for lectures. Why don't you tell me
what's bothering you while we have time left," he said.

I didn't know how to word it the right away. When
he coached me about life it felt strange because I
wasn't used to it, but being my dad, his words stuck
more.

"I know I got a job and all, and maybe someday I'll
meet the right girl, but I don't have too many friends
and there's never anything to do in Snydersville. I'm
getting scared about what I'm gonna do after school's
over. It seems like there's no future around here, but I

never want to be too far from you because I love you, Dad."

"I love you too, Pete but I don't think I'll be getting out of here anytime soon. There's a lot to do out there, kid. Maybe you don't know where to look?"

"I don't have any time to look."

"You're a young man now. Loosen up like one. Damn, Pete, you're too tense for a...how old are you now?"

"Seventeen."

"Seventeen years old? My God. It's time you start really living a little before it's all over and you're middle aged with a beer belly. You're past due on growing up and having a fun time. That's what people do in the free world. Check out those options life has put right before you and try out some new things, find out what you like to do."

"Like what? I mean what is there to do?"

"Do you drink yet?"

"I don't want to become an alcoholic like Troy."

"You are not the same person as Troy. He's dealing with his problems in the wrong way and that don't mean you can't enjoy a nice cold beer to get your mind off the hard days, occasionally. Do it as sort of a toast to me and next time you come for a visit, you can tell me what it tastes like. How it made you feel."

"Don't you know that already?"

My dad leaned in, his eyes locking onto mine like he was trying to reach into my soul through the glass that separated us. "Pete, you've got your whole life ahead of you. I can't be out there with you pointing the way, but you can bring a piece of the world back to me and describe it. You've got to live, son. Really live."

I looked down, my hands fidgeting in my lap. "It's not that easy, Dad."

"But it is," he insisted, his voice softening. "Life only gets complicated when we let it or we get in our own way. You're young, you're healthy, and you've got a job you like. That's more than a lot of people can say. Your circumstances don't define you."

I met his eyes again, feeling a strange mix of comfort and challenge in his gaze. He wanted to see me grow up and not make the same mistakes as himself. "So what would you do if you were me?"

His smile broke through, inspired and awakened like a ray of sunshine in this dreary place. "I want you to feel life, Pete. I want you to taste that first sip of beer, feel the sun on your face, kiss the girl, and then come back and tell me all about it. Make it so vivid that I can close my eyes and be there with you."

Something about the way he said it sent a shiver down my spine. I knew what he meant, but it felt like a challenge more than a good wish. "Alright, Dad. I'll do it. I'll start really living, and I'll make sure to share it all with you."

His eyes got narrow, and he nodded. "That's what I want to hear. Remember, we're not the sum of our circumstances. We're defined by what we do with the time we've got. And you've got some."

"I won't let you down, Dad. I promise."

He leaned back, looking satisfied. "Good. Now go out there and make some memories for both of us."

I nodded, my heart full, my mission clear. "I will, Dad. I totally will."

He looked up at the clock and noticed that red light was on and put his hand on the glass divider. I put mine on the other side as if we're touching. His hand was huge and rough compared to mine. Maybe I wasn't trying hard enough. Maybe he was right that I am holding back despite being a free man out here.

"OK, Dad. I'll do it for us and I'll report back to you about my adventures."

"Now that's more like it. Be happy son, because you've got all kinds of new experiences waiting ahead of you. All you gotta do is meet life halfway and the rest works itself out."

I saw the reflection of the guard open the door on my dad's side, standing behind him waiting for us to wrap it up. He looked back and nodded.

"You think I'll be seeing you again soon?"

"Probably next weekend, after I have my first cold one while watching the sunset."

"Good, son. I am looking forward to it. Just knowing you'll be doing that will make me smile in my cell at night."

"Thanks for the pep talk, Dad. I needed it."

"I'm always here for it," he said with a grin, then winked at me before standing up and facing the guard waiting with handcuffs to walk him back to his cell. I watched him shuffle off but didn't feel as sad as usual. He made me realize that I was surviving and not living like the free man that I am. With school coming to an end, I really could do anything with my time soon. I put my hands in my pockets and was led out of the visitation room by another guard.

I had a lot to think about on my bike ride back to Snydersville that day. I took the same way home but got tired at the halfway point and pushed my bike up to the top. There was a little area off the side of the road where I could rest and take in both valleys without being seen from the road. I leaned my bike against a giant weeping willow tree. Looking back at the prison, I knew I never wanted to ever end up there myself, but then I saw horses hanging out at the farm down the way realized they were in a similar situation as me—free but confined to a large area where they didn't notice.

As my eyes drifted between the prison and the horses, I thought about the concept of freedom. The horses, with their powerful legs and flowing manes, embodied a kind of freedom, yet they were confined to their fenced-in pastures. Was that so different from the life I was living? Confined by circumstances, by the town, by my family situation? Those were my pastures.

I thought about what my dad had said, about living life to the fullest and bringing those experiences back to him. It was a heavy responsibility, but also an opportunity to do something together in a weird way. An opportunity to break free, even if in small moments, from the boundaries that held us both back.

I picked up a small stone and tossed it down the hill, watching as it bounced and rolled, unrestricted, until it disappeared into the tall grass. I envied that stone, unburdened by thoughts or limitations. It went wherever gravity took it, while I had to navigate a maze of expectations and obstacles.

I stood up, dusting off my jeans, and looked once more at the prison in the distance. "Not me," I whispered to myself. "I won't end up there." I felt a new sense of determination fill me. I had a job that I liked, a dad who believed in me, and a whole world to explore. Maybe I wasn't completely free, but I was free enough to make my own choices.

I grabbed my bike and hopped back on, pedaling with a newfound energy. As I made my way down the hill, I thought about the beer I'd try, the sunrises I'd stop and take in, and the stories I'd bring back to my dad. The weight of my circumstances felt a little bit lighter that day.

As I rode into Snydersville, the town was a bit less confining, its boundaries a bit more spread out. My perspective had changed. I was still me, still Pete Mc-Closkey from a small town with its share of problems, but I was also someone who could dream, someone who could taste a bit of freedom and yearn for more. And that made all the difference.

MONDAY'S GLOOM

On my first day with a new attitude, the clouds were a thick quilt smothering the whole valley. It was the kind of weather that made you want to crawl back into bed, but instead, I found myself on the football field for gym class. Mr. Thume, our gym teacher, was in his element. The man looked like he'd been born in a vat of motor oil, with his slicked-back hair and Elvis-like sideburns. He wore jeans and a light blue work shirt, which clashed horribly with his pristine white gym sneakers. The whistle and stopwatch around his neck were the only indicators that he was, in fact, a gym teacher and not a mechanic who'd wandered onto the field by mistake.

We were doing squat thrusts on the damp turf, and it was a mess. Each thrust produced more face plants and belly flops than actual exercise. The girls, who were running laps around the track, slowed to watch our misery unfold, laughing as they did.

I couldn't help but watch Morgan as she effortlessly lapped her classmates, opting not to slow down. She was going for time and kept her pace until the end.

Mr. Thume's whistle cut through my daydream.

"Good! Now you fellas are that much closer to actually being in shape for adulthood," he said, his voice dripping with bar room sarcasm. We all panted, catching our breath as he continued his verbal assault. "You're free to hit the showers after you've all completed one hundred jumping jacks."

The collective groan that erupted sounded like something got slaughtered. Chad Parks, ever the loudmouth, couldn't help himself.

"What the heck is this, the National Guard or something? School's over soon you know."

Mr. Thume zeroed in on Chad like a hawk spotting its prey. He marched up to him, stopping inches from his face.

"You think I don't know that Parksy. It's my job to get you into shape and teach you some good habits before you move into your parents' basement for the rest of your life and that's what I do. Got that?"

Chad nodded, wiping his nose with the back of his hand like he was gearing up for a boxing match. He started his jumping jacks, and Mr. Thume stood right in front of him, counting aloud.

"One, two, three—come on, ladies, get synced up," he barked. "You look like a bunch of collapsing finger puppets, let's go."

I joined in on the jumping jacks, but my thoughts drifted back to Morgan, who was now stretching over on the bleachers with some other girls. She toweled off her face and looked at me and smiled. My posture became perfect. I was in the military now. I smiled back, all tough like until Thume's whistle broke the spell.

"Alright, ladies. Get on in and shower up. You smell like wet socks and B.O.," he barked the blew his whistle three more times. He loved that thing.

I hated taking a shower in school, but the water was hot and the soap was free except for shampoo so I did it.

The large shower room was all steamed up by the time I got undressed and walked in. There were a few posts with shower heads spread out. I found one nobody was at, pressed the button and lathered up. The water felt so good compared to the icicles that come out of the shower head at home. Chad, Will and couple of their friends were laughing it up across the way. I minded my own business and cleaned up as fast as I could. When I reached out to hit the off-button Will came over to me and offered some of his shampoo in a tiny Pert bottle.

"Sorry about before, McCloskey. Here. Take some of my shampoo, I don't need it."

I was suspicious but I did want to wash my hair with shampoo since I never did. I reached my hand out because he looked like he wanted to pour some for me and instead he dumped the bottle on my head, and I could smell and taste the urine mixed with soapy water. Laughter came at me through the steam as I hit that button so fast and started scrubbing my hair as hard as possible, then I put a huge amount of body soap in my hands and washed some more. The whole time I was gagging and spitting while everyone from class watched and laughed as word spread about what they did.

Mr. Thume came bursting from his little office to the shower area.

"Once you're cleaned you get out. Understand me? No horsing around in the shower, McCloskey."

I kept scrubbing while everyone left, and I didn't want to stop. I hated Chad and Will so much but together they would break my neck and I didn't have a big brother worth a damn to ever get my back. It sucked.

"McCloskey! What are you trying to do? Wash your hair right off? That's enough already."

I slammed the off button and faced him, water dripping down my forehead, I could see Chad and Will out in the locker room looking in, big grins, a gang of friends behind them all swallowing their laughter. Chad pointed at mouthed "Shhhh." while showing me a clenched fist.

I walked to the paper towel dispenser and punched the lever until I had enough of a wad to start drying myself. I was the only kid who didn't bring a towel to school on gym days because I only had one to my name. The rest of the class was dressed and lined up by the door when the bell rang, meaning I was going to be late for another class and get detention again. This is how every week went for me through the years and even now as school was coming to an end. I hated it but knew if I could make it, at least I'd have my diploma and better chance at life.

Detention was a cruel joke, a room with a view that taunted you with glimpses of your peers enjoying their after-school time. Situated on the ground floor, the classroom's windows faced the baseball fields and the student parking lot, a constant reminder of what you were missing, namely the ability to flee. It felt like a rehearsal for jail, and the irony wasn't lost on me. I hated letting Mr. Stilson down, but he knew what my life was like, so I had to suck it up and endure the injustice for now.

Ricky was a detention regular, racking up in-school suspensions and after-school detentions like they were badges of honor. We used to hang out back in 6th and 7th grade, but life got in the way; his mom passed away and my dad got put away, and we drifted apart. As we walked out of the school together, the parking lot was empty and silent. Mrs. James, the detention monitor, exited behind us, gave us both a see you tomorrow scowl, before turning towards the lot. She was a stern-faced woman who wielded her power like a weapon, adding extra nights of detention as she saw fit.

I watched Ricky, with an unlit cigarette dangling from his lips, give her a two-handed salute of middle fingers as she walked away. It made me laugh. He fumbled for his lighter, finally igniting his cigarette and taking a long drag.

"Man, we gotta hang out again before school's over, Pete. This is it, you know? No more summers of only fun," Ricky said, exhaling a cloud of smoke.

"I know, man. Time's flying. I've been swamped with work, trying to save every penny I can," I replied.

"I heard that tubalard Will Cleveland pissed in a shampoo bottle then gave it to you. You shouldn't let that slide, man. Together, we could kick his ass if we wanted to, a final beat down to end school," Ricky suggested, a glint of mischief in his eyes.

"I can't afford to get into trouble. My focus is on getting out of Troy's hellhole and starting my own life," I said, locking eyes with his one good eye.

Ricky nodded, taking another drag from his cigarette. "Yeah, I get it. But you know, Pete, sometimes you gotta fight for your right to exist, even if it's only from assholes like Chad and Will that don't want you to for some dumb reason."

"It's not worth it, man."

"Well, if you're serious about moving out on your own, maybe we could be roommates. We could throw parties every night!"

"We'd probably end up at the bars, accomplishing nothing," I said, pushing my bike alongside Ricky as we walked down the sidewalk.

"That's the whole point of being an adult, isn't it?" Ricky retorted, flicking his cigarette butt into the street. "You work and accomplish nothing, then you party all night. Then you get old and die."

"It doesn't have to be. That's the Snydersville way."

"So what else is there? Besides working and drinking, I'm drawing a blank," Ricky said, resigning himself to his own low expectations.

"I've been at Stilson's for three years now, started when I was 14. It's not bad," I said, steering the conversation away from the depressing reality of our town.

"Three years? Man, you must have a treasure trove of booze at your place by now. Johnny Walker, JD, Wild Turkey..." Ricky mused, his eyes lighting up at the thought.

"No way. Troy would guzzle it all down in one night, and I don't want to help him do more damage to himself. So, I steer totally clear."

Ricky stopped walking and looked at me, his expression a cocktail of disbelief and disappointment. "Are you kidding me? If I worked at a liquor store, I'd have enough secret stash to open my own bar by now. You get all the breaks but don't know how to use 'em. Hey, you up for something wild tonight?"

My gut reaction was to decline, like I'd been doing since ninth grade. But then I remembered my dad's words about embracing my freedom while I'm young. I'd never really done anything wild, and it felt overdue.

"I'm working until nine. What's the plan?" I said, mounting my bike, ready to pedal off.

"It's a surprise. Meet me at the middle school basketball courts after you close up. And bring some booze to make it fun night. You're gonna like this, Pete," Ricky said, rubbing his hands together like a cartoon villain plotting his next move.

"Alright, I'll be there. But it better not be anything illegal," I warned, feeling a mix of anticipation and apprehension.

"Oh don't worry, you'll see. It's gonna be epic," Ricky assured me, his one straight eye twinkling with mischief.

We parted ways but Ricky said the magic words that made me commit: "we gotta live a little" and I took that as a sign.

I pedaled fast to get to work. The whole way there I was thinking about how Ricky sounded a lot like my dad. I have been holding back the past few years, while many of my friends have been drunk and gotten laid, I was living the same monotonous routine. Always thinking about the future me which was just out of reach in my imagination.

Ricky and I were always together when we were younger, and I missed having nothing to do but hang out like in those simple days. Ever since I started working my summers haven't been the same. I needed to change that quickly before work is all that I do.

When I got to the liquor store, Stilson looked at me over the top of his glasses.

"I know. I'm late," I said.

"What happened this time?"

"Guilt by association." I told him while tying my work apron on.

"Good thing that's not going to be an issue in a few more weeks," he said.

"No sir. I will be glad to be done with school and most of the people in it."

"You don't have any good friends, Pete?"

"I used to...but, ya know-"

"Listen Pete, I do know. We all got to go through bad times. Most of my friends went to Nam and never came back the same. Your generation is facing different wars but they're still wars. And us folks up here in the rust belt, we're on the front lines of changing economic times."

"Why didn't you go to Nam if so many of your friends did?"

"Right before my draft notice arrived, I got in a car wreck that shattered my leg and kept me out. I went to to work for the post office, then when my case was settled, I invested the insurance money and then used the profits to start this business and have been doing it ever since. It was a lucky break, but it didn't feel that way at first. I wanted to go and fight with my friends but I'm glad I never got to."

I looked at Stilson differently. I didn't see "old man Stilson" with his limp, I saw a guy who lucked out by having bad luck first. I knew bad luck followed me like a shadow on a sunny day and I wondered what I might be getting saved from, if anything at all, during this long run of bad luck in my life. At least I hoped I was. For the rest of my shift, I restocked cases of beer, swept out the parking lot of cigarette butts and litter. The whole time I was thinking about Stilson's friends who got drafted and that I was going to take up Ricky on his invite, so I don't miss out on being young. We had that in common. Stolen youth was a theme many had to deal with around here and I didn't realize it.

Mr. Stilson noticed me nosing around the liquor bottles and it's like he knew I was thinking of taking one.

"You looking for something in particular?" he said

standing behind me. I turned around fast, guilty of the thought but he expected it because every teenager around town drinks booze on the regular. Well, everyone but me.

"Yeah, um, my brother wanted to know if I could bring home a bottle of Absolute for his birthday."

"Your brother has a drinking problem, Pete. Everyone knows it. Besides, I can't sell alcohol to a minor. And I know you wouldn't be getting your drunk brother more of what's bad for him. What are really you up to? Is there a girl?"

"Just hanging out ya know, trying to have a little fun while we still can before it's all over. I can pay you for it. What if I put in my book bag? I'm heading straight home from here. No one will ever know."

Stilson sensed I was up to something. I could tell he didn't think less of me for asking. He knew my story as well as anyone and probably felt sorry for me even though he didn't treat me that way. I knew he understood because he grew up here too; getting drunk with friends under a bridge or out in the woods is a rite of passage which morphs into a bad habit for too many.

"Only one bottle this one time? Nobody's operating a car who's drinking it?" he said.

"No sir," I said and pulled some cash from the small inside pocket on my jeans where I kept emergency cash wadded up. He pushed my hand down.

"Put your money away. This one is on the house. Consider it an early graduation present," he said while handing me the bottle and nodding his head to tell me to take it to the back room where my bike and bag was.

"Thanks Mr. Stilson. I owe you one. Big time."

I went to the back and slipped the bottle into my

backpack, nestling it among all the loose papers and dirty gym clothes. When I came back, he was looking out the front window with both arms crossed like he was in deep thought.

"I've been thinking about your schedule. Why don't you go ahead and take the weekends off from now on," he said.

"From now on, like forever?"

"That's right but there's one catch," he said.

"Name it."

"Stay on and work for me full time after your graduate. Monday through Friday."

"Full time like from like nine-to-five every day?"

"More like nine-to-nine. I'm getting too old for this Pete. I need to rest and enjoy my grandkids more and we'll hire a helper for you. I'd work on the weekends so you can be free. A hard-working young man like you needs a couple of days off."

I didn't know what to say and stood there looking at him.

"You don't have to give me an answer right now. Think about it because it's a commitment that I would expect you to keep if you agree. I need someone to take over Pete. You're a good kid and I trust you."

"Alright Mr. Stilson. I'll think about it and let you know."

As I wheeled my bike out into the night after we closed, the sky opened up, each constellation twinkling a little brighter, a little closer than before. A small sense of fun settled over me. I looked back at Stilson's modest brick building, standing alone in the parking lot beside the highway, and felt a wave of gratitude. College was never in the cards for me, but here I was, with a job and a future. I had the basics down, and that was enough. Tonight felt like the beginning of something new, a return to living, not just existing.

I mounted my bike, my thoughts buzzing with anticipation. My dad was right; I had been living too cautiously for someone my age. I was lagging, but not for long. Tonight was about catching up, about reclaiming lost moments.

I pedaled over the bridge connecting North Snydersville to the main town, and the roads were as empty as ever, save for a lone, jacked up pickup truck whose AC/DC soundtrack could be heard in the air. The truck hesitated at a red light before roaring off into the distance. I took a left past the high school, following a side street that ran along the riverbank and led to the middle school. The houses I passed were dimly lit, almost as if they were holding their breath, waiting for something to happen. The only signs of life were the occasional barks of a dog or the creaking slam of a screen door.

At the end, the road curved right, running parallel to the river and leading me into another neighborhood where the middle school stood like a relic from a bygone era. Unlike the high school, with its cold, institutional feel, the middle school was built of old brick with white trim, its architecture detailed and inviting. It was a building from a time when people took pride in their work and community, and it showed.

I circled the school's parking lot, weaving in and out of the beam of light that half-illuminated the basketball court. I straddled my bike and waited for Ricky. There were voices coming from a shaded area near the back of the court, so I rode towards it. A glass beer bottle came rolling towards me from the darkness. I stopped and stood there straddling my bike.

"Who's that?" said a voice.

"It's McCloskey. I got some vodka."

"What the fuck are you doing here, scumbag?"

Chad and Will emerged from the shadows and went right for my backpack. I tried to get away but Will held the handlebars and kept pushing at my forehead while Chad found the bottle of vodka in my bag.

"Where you going little weirdo? Killer's son. Loser. I heard your daddy is getting fucked up the ass by a big coon up in Mapleton right and you got a new momma, Jo Mamma," he said, then shoved me backwards. I lost balance and ended up on the ground while Chad walked away with the vodka in hand and let all my books and papers fall out.

"Citron, nice." I heard him say as they walked back into the shadows where a bench was that you could barely see. At least they were preoccupied with the vodka, leaving me a second to grab my stuff and get out of there. I stuffed all the papers and books back in, lifted my bike, turned it around and hopped on, pissed at Ricky for setting me up. I pedaled around the school to cut through the front lawn and when I passed a row of hedges I heard a familiar voice.

"Well, there goes our booze," said Ricky.

I hit the brakes and leaned towards the bushes.

"Ricky?"

"Get in here, McCloskey so those jerks can't see us," said Ricky.

I spread apart the branches and saw Ricky and our friend Little T. sitting on a large rock, illuminated from the streetlight on the corner.

"Hey why didn't you come help me when you saw them stealing the vodka I brought for you?" I whispered.

Little T. was nervous and bit his fingernails. Ricky looked down and spit some brown chaw water and then looked back out towards the area where Chad and Will were.

"It would have been two on one, and I am not in the mood for that. T don't fight and you hit like a girl for all I know."

"I never hit anyone before."

"Exactly."

I huddled down next to them. "So. What are we doing here? What are they doing here?"

"You don't know about Amanda Breyer?" whispered Little T. He was the shy kid brother of Big Tyrone, a local football legend who got killed a few years back when his Trans Am rolled into a ditch and he and his girlfriend died. Nobody would mess with Little T. He had football legend protection but I, on the other hand did not.

"Amanda Breyer? My brother's ex-girlfriend from high school?"

"That's the one," said Little T.

"Troy used to date her?" Asked Ricky.

"Yeah, a long time ago. She's used to come up to my house all the time. What about her? I never see her anywhere around town."

Ricky looked past me over to the bench area where Chad and Will were taking turns drinking the vodka, getting drunk and louder.

"You don't know what she does for money? She gets banged, McCloskey. She's a bar room hooker and every night her window over there is wide open and it's like free a porno show," said Ricky while rubbing his hands together all giddy like.

"No way," I said.

"Way," said Little T. with a big grin. "I've seen it."

"You're still a virgin aren't you McCloskey?" pressed Ricky.

"Holy fuck, I'm drunk," said Chad from across the way. We all looked in that direction. They didn't pace themselves and got hammered in a matter of minutes.

"Hold up...I think they're leaving," said T.

I peeked out as Will swayed half in the light and half in the shadow with his head back, chugging the vodka straight down like Troy. He stopped abruptly, passed the bottle to Chad and yakked all over the parking lot while Chad stumbled nearby laughing at his friend's vomit show.

"You fuckin' lightweight," said Chad.

"They're either leaving or passing out," said Ricky.

"If they pass out, I'm gonna go pee all over them before I go home," I said.

"I'll drop a deuce right on Will's fat face," said Ricky.

"They're leaving," said Little T.

"I wonder if they came here to watch too because I've never seen them here before," said Ricky.

"Wait. How long have you been coming here to watch Amanda have sex?"

"A couple of weeks is all. I was cutting through her backyard one night when I saw what I saw and since then I had to confirm it before telling you guys. T came with me the second time because I ran into him down to the rec center," said Ricky.

"Which one is her house?" I said, looking through the branches to the row of old houses that lined the street across from the school. I knew Amanda was hot. She and Troy were high school sweethearts, but then after the incident that sent my dad to jail, I never saw her again.

"She rents the ground floor of that brown one, fourth house from the riverbank," said Ricky.

"When does this show start because I don't wanna hang out under this tree all night," I said.

"Yeah, Ricky. When's she coming home?" said Little T.

"What time is it?" asked Ricky.

"It's probably like ten by now," I said.

A lone set of headlights lit up the street as a pickup truck turned in and drove to the third house from the riverbank and pulled into the driveway. We all watched with bated breath as a man and woman, both drunk and giggling, kissed and groped each other all the way to the front door. The moonlight was bright enough to see their faces and it was Amanda all right and she was still as beautiful as I remembered. She took the man by the hand and pulled him up the stairs. She opened the door, and they smooched some more right in the doorway before practically falling inside together.

Ricky grabbed my shoulder all excited like. "It's showtime. C'mon, there's a hidden spot between houses where we can see everything bro, everything."

"What about my bike?"

"Leave it here. Nobody can see it," said Little T.

We moved the branches and crawled out from under the tree and stayed close to the school shadows until we reached the bench where Chad and Will were before. Ricky led us across the street and we slipped into the dark area between the two houses. Amanda's had one large side window that looked right into her living room and there were no curtains. The house beside it had no windows, so I understood why she didn't think about covering up. We took positions against the other house and were basically standing in pitch blackness.

It was weird seeing her all grown up and naked

since I knew Amanda from way back when life was good and my family was in one piece. She and Troy were like peanut butter and jelly back then but now she was an adult woman it was like I was seeing her for the first time. She let the guy who came home with her undress her. He sat down on her couch and started kissing and sucking on her breasts while she played with his hair.

"Look at them titties," Little T. said too loud and quickly covered his own mouth.

"Oh man she gives me such a big boner baby," whispered Ricky.

"Them boobies is luscious. I would suck those all day," added Little T.

"Stop talking you guys." I hushed them both and then we all watched in slack-jawed silence as Amanda Breyer, someone I have known my whole life as a responsible person, have sex with this drunk dude on her couch.

She laid back and he did his thing. She moaned and he did too. The show was over fast though. Once they laid down and started humping it was over and I swear she looked in our direction. We ducked out and ran across the street to the school, giggling nervously after seeing live sex. I grabbed my bike and pushed as we walked the dimly lit streets of town.

"That was freakin' crazy, man. Crazy!" I said.

"Maybe next time you'll see her do the other stuff," said Ricky.

"Like what?" I said.

"BJ's," stated Little T.

"She's good at it too," said Ricky.

"She does this every night?" I asked.

"Every night probably. She's a pro," said Ricky.

"I didn't know she had that many boyfriends," I said.

Ricky turned around and started walking backwards so he could talk directly to us.

"McCloskey, have you been living under a rock? Do you even know what she does for a living? What a pro is? This is her job, not some hobby."

I really didn't know. I shook my head side to side.

"She's a hooker. Anyone can pay to have sex with her."

"Anyone?" I pressed.

"Anyone," said Ricky and Little T. at the same time.

"And you got a job, McCloskey," said Ricky, eyebrow up, as he pulled out his smokes and fished for another cigarette.

"Amanda was the homecoming queen and the most popular girl in my brother's class. Why would a beautiful girl who could get any guy, do that?" I said.

"Easy money," said Little T.

"World's oldest profession," added Ricky.

I thought about it. While it didn't look like easy money, it didn't look like hard work either. It looked like they both liked it, but only Amanda got paid.

At the end of the neighborhood we hit Main Street. Little T. lived a few blocks down. Ricky and I resided on the other side of the tracks. Before we split, we made plans to hang out more, to reclaim some of the time we'd lost.

I hopped on my bike and pedaled home at a leisurely pace, my mind replaying the sound of Amanda's moans. It was a sound I'd never heard in real life before—strange, yet pleasantly intoxicating, calling from a world I was only beginning to understand.

As I cycled through the quiet streets, I pondered my dad's words, contemplating the newfound freedom that lay before me. One thing was clear: I wanted a life that included someone like Amanda who wanted to be with me for me. That meant having a job, money, and no more Troy to hold me back.

I reached the bridge that led to my hill but felt too restless to head straight home. Instead, I pulled my bike up onto the riverbank to think and look at the stars. Across the water lay Amanda's apartment, and it struck me how the geography of our lives was so interconnected yet divided. Troy would descend the hill to the bars, while Amanda would emerge from her apartment to the same destination. In towns like Snydersville, all roads lead to the bars, as if they were gravitational centers pulling in lives that had come to a standstill.

In that moment, I knew I never wanted to be ensnared in a stagnant lifestyle, where the days blurred into nights and years slipped away unnoticed. The factory lights from the railroad depot shimmered on the river's calm smooth surface, turning the whole scene into a glittering dreamscape. The night was cool but not cold, and I stayed there for a long time, lost in thought. I knew that when I got home, Troy would be passed out somewhere, a living embodiment of the life I was determined to avoid.

So, I sat there, on the edge of the river, on the cusp of adulthood, feeling as if I were on the brink of something profound but I had no clue what it was that awaited me.

FALLING HARD

I woke up and decided to inform Mr. Stilson about accepting the full-time job after high school. Taking a shortcut through town, I found myself passing Morgan Downer's house. She was in her front yard, cleaning up a small flower bed to make way for spring flowers. She stood up and waved. As I glanced back to see who she was waving to, my focus faltered and my tire collided with the curb, sending my right foot careening off the pedal. Momentum swung my leg around, gouging a painful chunk from my knee as I toppled over, face-first, onto her lawn. The sting in my knee was agonizing, eclipsed only by the humiliation of sprawling in front of her. My forehead survived with minor scuffs, but my pride? That was another story. I looked totally stupid.

Morgan rushed over, her eyes wide with concern. "Oh my God, are you okay?"

I tried to muster a grin through the grimace, probably looking like I was having a facial spasm. She knelt beside me, her hair cascading over her forehead, partially veiling her face, a look that made her even more mysterious to me.

"We need to clean this before it gets infected," she declared.

"Yep," was all I managed to utter.

"Let's get you inside."

Hobbling toward her porch, I clung to her shoulder, my knee pulsating with pain, my stomach knotted with embarrassment nerves.

Her mom appeared at the door, eyes widening at the sight. "Oh dear, that looks nasty," she said, holding the screen door ajar.

"Come inside. I'll grab the first-aid kit," Morgan instructed.

Blood dripped onto the porch as I pressed my jeans against the wound. "I shouldn't bleed all over your house," I said, opting for the porch swing.

Her mom examined the gash. "It's not terrible, but it needs attention."

Morgan burst through the door, first-aid kit in hand. She deftly used bobby pins to pin back my torn jeans, then dabbed the wound with a white washcloth —now destined for the trash. I tried to help, but she pushed my hands away.

"Morgan's pre-med, aiming for pediatrics," her mom beamed.

"Really?" I winced. "Impressive."

"Brace yourself," Morgan warned, applying hydrogen peroxide to the wound. I bit my lip, gripping the swing's armrests, determined not to yelp like a weakling. The initial sting subsided, replaced by the soothing touch of ointment and a sterile bandage. My knee still throbbed, but that was a minor inconvenience now.

"It's probably going to hurt for a few days. You must keep cleaning it out or it could get infected," she said while looking up at me. She turned her head to the right and spotted my bike, always one step ahead of everything.

"You probably don't want to ride your bike for the rest of the day. I can give you a ride," Morgan offered, her mom handing her the keys and a small wad of cash.

"Nah, I'm good. Wasn't heading home anyway. A walk might actually do the leg some good."

I tried to stand, but a jolt of pain shot through my leg, making me wince. Morgan caught it, offering her shoulder for support.

"Mom, can you put his bike in the trunk?"

"This is so embarrassing," I muttered.

"Don't sweat it. I was about to run errands anyway. I'll drop you off."

Carefully, I eased into the back seat of their silver Chevette. Her mom managed to fit my bike in the trunk, leaving it slightly ajar. The backseat was a mini menagerie of stuffed animals and trinkets, all staring at me like quiet spectators. Awkward? Hell, yes. But there was something about Morgan's energy—calming, different. It was as if her vibe had a way of seeping into you, making the awkwardness bearable, even welcome.

"Where were you heading, Pete?"

"I, uh...was going to see an old friend. I should probably go home instead, probably shouldn't try and make it worse."

"You live on the south side of the tracks, " she said after starting the car.

"Up on Dobes Hill. Last house."

"I'm going to stop at the drugstore on the way. Is that okay with you?" Morgan asked.

"Yeah, sure, no problem," I replied, my eyes meeting hers in the rearview mirror. She was angelic, both in looks and actions. The thought of her seeing the mess I called home made me cringe on the inside, but walking all the way up that hill was out of the question.

"Pete?" She glanced at me again while driving.

"Huh?"

"What's your plan after graduation?"

I froze for a moment. I didn't really have a plan, only a trajectory and it was the only one I knew how to follow.

"Sticking with Stilson's. Might even become the night manager."

"Running a liquor store, huh? That what you want out of life?"

"It's not bad, you know? I like the people, and it's a job. What about you? When did you decide on pediatrics?" I needed to steer the conversation away from me.

"My little sister, Kayla. She died from pediatric cancer and that changed everything in my new family. I'm going to find a cure one day."

Her words hit me like a ton of bricks. I sank deeper into the backseat. It was a revelation to me that pain and suffering didn't discriminate. Suddenly, Morgan wasn't the angelic figure who had her life in control; she was human, like me, shaped by life's cruel twists that directed her path.

"I'm so sorry. I never knew that, Morgan. And we've been in the same grade and classes forever."

"Not many people do. Remember my absence for most of sixth grade?"

"Yeah, you even missed the class picture that year."

"That was the year she died," she said softly. "My mom's never been the same. My poor dad, he never coped and died of a broken heart. That's why I'm picking up my mom's antidepressants now. It's been hard."

My problems felt small compared to hers and I felt even smaller in that moment. Morgan pulled over and parked in front of Rite Aid and glanced back at me.

"I'll be quick."

"Take your time. I'm not going anywhere," I said with a half-smile.

As I lay there, her story filled the gaps in my understanding of why she was the way she was. Her drive, her excellence—they weren't just traits; they were born from love and loss she experienced at a young age. She had a purpose, something I couldn't say for myself. My only purpose was to survive, but hers was driven by a desire to right the wrongs, to put back together what was broken, and in that moment I knew that Morgan was someone I related too much more than I thought.

She returned and started the car back up. "Top of Dobes Hill, right?"

"Yeah."

She nodded, and we continued driving. I found myself staring out the back window, captivated by the tops of old buildings that made up the small strip of downtown Snydersville. From this angle, the town didn't look as depressing as it usually did. The treetops, rooftops, and open sky hinted at a past glory and a potential future. But then we crossed the bridge, passing the bars and the scenery changed. The houses looked even more run-down than those in other parts of town. I sat up straighter and spoke as she drove up Dobes Hill and we were about halfway up.

"Could you pull over and let me out here please?" I asked, not wanting her to see the state of my home and how gross it looked.

"Are you sure?" Morgan questioned.

"Please, Morgan. Let me out here," I insisted.

She looked at me through the rearview mirror, and I could tell she sensed I was hiding something. She pulled over to the side of the road and helped me get my bike out of the trunk. We stood there for an awkward moment.

"Thanks again. I was lucky you were there today," I said, grateful but also still totally embarrassed.

"I'm sure you'd do the same for me," she replied.

"I'd do anything for you, Morgan. I'd carry you home on one leg if I had to," I blurted out, immediately realizing how strange it must have sounded. She smiled at me.

"I mean, I would do anything for you after the way you've been helping me," I added, freezing for a moment with a goofy smile on my face.

"Pass your remedial math exam and graduate, and we'll call it even. You're a lot smarter than you let on, Pete," she said, encouragingly.

"Me and numbers, we're not exactly friends, but I'll give it a try," I responded.

"I know you can do it. Don't forget to keep that wound clean," she advised before getting back in her car, making a K-turn, and driving away down the hill, waving goodbye.

"I could love you, Morgan," I whispered to myself as I waved goodbye. She had cared for me today in a way that reminded me of how my mom used to care for me—a feeling I had forgotten but deeply missed. The wounds of life are kept clean by love so they can heal and become scars. Morgan was right that we have to keep them clean, or they get worse.

I turned my bike around and began the slow, painful trek up the hill. As I pushed myself to the top, my thoughts kept returning to what my purpose in life could be. I yearned for more of that feeling I had experienced—the feeling of caring for someone and being cared for by someone. That's what love is and the more I thought about Morgan and what had happened between us today, the less I noticed the pain in my knee.

I reached my driveway, turned around, and with new eyes, took a long reflective look at the town I live in. The Catholic church steeple stood tall, rising above the buildings and bars. It was as if Snydersville was cradled in the valley and watched over by some higher power that kept each of us torn between our desires and our needs. As I stood there, staring at the steeple piercing the sky, it struck me how it was both a beacon and a warning. A beacon calling us to something higher, something pure, yet a warning that even in its shadow lay the broken homes and the bars, the places where people sought refuge when life became too much. It was like the valley itself was a metaphor for the human soul—full of contradictions, a battleground between our better angels and our inner demons. The church and the bars, they were like the two poles of a magnet, pulling us in opposite directions. And here we were, all of us in Snydersville, suspended in the tension between them. I thought about how easy it was to judge people like Troy, who appeared to have given in to their darker impulses. But then, who was I to judge? Wasn't I also a creature of this valley, battling between the person I wanted to be and the circumstances that tried to define me? In that moment, I felt a strange sense of unity with everyone in Snydersville, even those who never liked me. We were all navigating this rusting terrain of human existence, each in our own way. And maybe that's what the higher power watching over the valley was trying to teach us—that the journey was about learning to balance, to live in the tension between our desires and our needs, and to find our own path through the valley to the true things.

I pushed my bike into the garage, and as I passed by the side window, I saw Troy on the couch, drinking alone, surrounded by empty beer cans. It was going to be one of those nights—the worst kind, when he stayed home and drank alone. I always kept spare inner tubes and a tire patching kit in the garage. I flipped my bike upside down and set to work right there in the yard. The day was turning out to be quite pleasant, made even more so by my run in with Morgan. I felt a new desire to work harder on everything, to try and be smarter, and to take better care of myself. As I was changing the tire, my eyes caught sight of some words carved into the side of the English oak tree that stood between our house and the neighbor's property. It read, "Troy loves Amanda 4 Ever." I remembered how they used to be so in love, always holding hands and stealing kisses. I never understood the complexities of love—how it can be incredibly beautiful but also bring immense pain. I understood that I had been living my life in a way that allowed me to avoid both extremes. But now, I wasn't so sure that was how I wanted to continue.

MOTHS AND
BUTTERFLIES

Lying in bed as Troy got hammered downstairs listening to a Yankees game, memories I thought I'd buried deep resurfaced, filling my mind: the incomprehensible unraveling of my family. I was 12 when it happened, a moment forever etched in my memory, occurring in the predawn hours of a hot summer night.

Up until that point, my life had been what I considered normal. My parents were married, and my dad's railroad job took him out of town sporadically. When he was home, he'd take my brother Troy fishing at Loon Lake over the summer, both returning with sunburned faces and wide grins. But that night, time stood still. My dad returned from work a day early and was going to surprise my mom when he found another man in bed with her. My mom had a boyfriend —actually, as we'd later discover, she had several. But this one time, she got caught. They were asleep, naked and completely unaware of the storm that was about to hit.

Fury took over my dad. The house exploded with violence and shouting. He dragged the man out of bed and beat him to death in our driveway. Troy and I watched the horror unfold from our bedroom window, the police lights casting eerie shadows on the walls. I remember the sight of my dad being handcuffed and led away, the paramedics covering the lifeless body with a sheet, and my mom collapsing to the ground, sobbing uncontrollably in her bathrobe.

Witnessing it was surreal and made my body tingle with adrenaline like watching a gruesome movie play out in real life. A police counselor held Troy and me in our bedroom as they spoke to my mom. From that point on, a cloud of darkness landed on our home, a cloud that never lifted. The days and months that followed grew increasingly bleak and our lives changed.

My dad's sister Aunt Jess, already grappling with diabetes, moved in to help my mom raise us. While my aunt worked hard to keep life as normal as possible, my mom juggled with lawyers, investigators and psychiatrists too. She tried to overdose on prescription pills two times. And then one day she was gone. She took her car and left with a few items and nobody in all of Snydersville knew where she went. Rumor is she was in Vegas, working at a casino and living alone in a trailer park somewhere. Troy wished and hoped she's dead, but I can't do that. Either way, she left us to fend for ourselves, but really, she left me to Troy and that's what hurt the most.

Aunt Jess stayed with us up until Troy turned 18 and could legally become my guardian. Soon after leaving, she moved into a senior living home and passed away too, her condition taking its final toll on her. It became a recurring theme in my life: every good beginning inevitably led to a sudden and tragic end. I found myself wishing for a different past, one where my dad had more self-control, where he hadn't come home early that fateful night, and where my mom hadn't cheated on him.

In the animal kingdom it's only butterflies and moths that don't get parental care. Right at birth they're left to fend for themselves in a hostile and unforgiving environment. I wondered, does a moth know it's a moth? Does a butterfly know it's a butterfly? What I knew is that people can become either. Troy is like a moth drawn to an old flame that keeps getting burned. I wanted to become a butterfly and fly away, but deep down I knew I was moth material too. It unsettled me, so I tried not to think about it much more. I had work to do, wounds to keep clean and new life where I loosen up and live a little before I get old and die unhappy too.

I looked down at my knee and the bandage was so neatly put on that I didn't want to ever take it off. It was like Morgan patched my knee and now my heart stopped leaking and the blood was suddenly making me feel things again. The sky outside was bluer than usual, and a sense of possibility landed on me from nowhere. I fell asleep hard, dreaming about a different timeline where I was Morgan's high school sweetheart and her little sister Kayla never died. I wanted to put broken things back together again somehow.

My knee exploded when Troy whacked it with an old rolled up magazine, jolting me from sleep. He was standing at the end of the bed with his shirt off, drunk but not yet hammered, and his hair slicked back, looking ready to beat me with the magazine. He sipped from his beer bottle as I curled up, holding my throbbing knee with some fresh blood stains because he smashed it so hard.

"What the heck Troy! Leave me alone."

"What happened to your knee sissy?"

"I crashed on my bike and then you smashed it asshole. What happened to your face?"

And that was all it took for him to come after me. I slid right off my side and hobbled around the bed to avoid him.

"I need more money," demanded Troy. We were on opposite side of the bed now in a standoff that I have been in too many times to count. Troy wants what he wants and will beat me if he doesn't get it. That's why I keep my money hidden off property and not in the house.

"I already paid you this month and I don't got no more until next week."

"Give me the money and I won't break your other knee right here."

"You don't have to talk to me like that, ya know. I'm not stupid. I know you're a desperate drunk who no-body loves. You should try feeling that pain without the booze, you coward."

Troy pointed the rolled-up magazine at me and looked weaker and hurt by what I said, his fire fizzling fast.

"You don't know shit about being hard up. All you have to worry about is getting to school and your stupid little pussy ass job on time. You think you're cool because you work for old man Stilson?" he said.

"It's a job."

"Old man Stilson is like every other sick kiddie-diddler in this town, attracted to little boys like you. You should find out what he did to Bryce Wayland back in the day that made Bryce jump off the train track trestle and die. You'll see."

I shook my head. "No. That's not true. He's not like that and you shouldn't say stuff about people you don't even talk to or know."

"You should cough up some cash if you know what's good for you," he demanded and then started flipping my room looking for my stash.

"What are you going to do when I move out? Huh? What then?"

"You ain't going nowhere just like the rest of us. You're stuck here."

"I don't have to live with you after I'm 18. And I have a job so I can do what I want. Then what'll you do without me huh? I have freedom. What do you got besides an excuse and an addiction?"

Troy was mentally unstable and could turn hot and then cold in an instant. But I also knew how to hurt him in a way he couldn't defend against. It was my only way to stop his aggression. His expression turned sad, and he sat down on the end of the bed, head down, wringing the magazine in his hands. I felt sorry for him because he did have a good job right out of high school, working construction up in Rochester right after our dad was sent to prison and our mom left us.

Then one day I come home from school and he's sitting on the couch with a back and neck brace on, getting drunk in the middle of the day. The back injury left him with a permanent swagger that looked like he was leaning away slightly at all times, too cool for anyone. But then, Troy's entire life became about collecting his disability and insurance payments which were always magically tied up in paperwork at some lawyer's office downtown. The case went on, he got better, the case went on, he drank his time away while living on unemployment, the case went on and on and one day he's going to get compensation and start his new life. At least that's what he always told me. He centered his whole life on that money which never came and now with time running out he's skimming from me, getting desperate and mean.

"I've applied for every job I see in the paper, Pete. I can't even get even get hired at the grocery store around here with our last name," he said.

"It sucks being a McCloskey, I know. I get shit about it all the time," I said.

"Well fuck the world if they don't like us. Fuck everyone, Pete."

"There are good people out there."

"Well fuck this town then. There ain't none here," he said.

"Troy, you smell like booze all the time. I bet that has something to do with you not getting hired."

"You don't fucking know what it's like, kid. You should mind your own business."

He downed the last of his beer and hurled the bottle at the wall next to me. Instead of shattering, it merely clinked against the wall and rolled onto the floor in a pathetic way. In that moment, I saw vulnerability cross his face. The bottle's refusal to break on his command mirrored his own internal fragility, as if both were too messed up to even fall apart properly.

"Fuuuuuuuck!" said Troy as he held his head in his hands and started sobbing. I never witnessed him this weak before. He stopped talking to me like I was his brother a long time ago and this was the first moment we weren't yelling or fighting to communicate. His shoulders were slumped forward and the Iron Maiden tattoo on his left shoulder looked like Eddie was enjoying every bit of Troy's pain. Laughing at him with that wicked looking smile, those illuminated eyes. Troy had a couple of heavy metal tattoos on his back and arms, and they all mocked him every time I found him face down in his own vomit, crashed out on the floor.

"Aren't you sick of always scrounging for money, always being desperate?" I asked.

"Hell yes I'm fuckin' sick of being broke and want my damn settlement check so I can move on from it all," he said.

"We're broke in more ways than one. Money can't fix this," I said.

"You think I don't know that?"

"Go see Dad. Seriously. He asked about you. He'll talk you straight."

Troy turned his head at me, eyes watery but no tears, only bitterness.

"I don't ever want to see that motherfucker again," he said then stood up, steeled himself and left my room. I heard him head down the stairs.

"Where are you going?" I yelled out.

"Fuck off, Pete."

"Love you too, bro."

And then I heard him banging around for a few minutes before the front door slammed open and then shut.

I turned around and watched him walk down our hill wearing his jeans, a t-shirt and his Carhartt jacket. He looked pissed and on a mission, but I knew he was heading into town to get as drunk as possible to erase another day because he always had a little bit of drinking money laying around, somehow.

While I cleaned up the mess he made, I heard some banging on the front door but couldn't see who it was from up here. I went down and opened the door seeing Ricky and Little T. standing down on the sidewalk.

"What are you guys doing up here?" I said.

"We're going to check out if the old fort is still up because we got some weed," said Little T. "You wanna come?"

"Where'd you get pot?" I asked.

"My cousin. He gave me this whole joint," he said while flashing the rolled smoke at me that was hidden under his hand.

What was going to be a day of committing to my future at Stilson's and then another visit with Dad, turned into an encounter with Morgan that got me thinking, a small win against Troy's harassment and now an adventure to try a new experience like he said I needed. Pot wasn't used by a lot of people that I knew of back then. Snydersville was a booze town to the core but there was a small circle of pot heads, and they didn't bother anyone. "Hang on, I gotta get my shoes," I said.

I came out and closed the door behind me. Our old fort was about a one-mile hike into the woods back behind my house and the three of us hadn't been back there in years. Ricky noticed my bloody knee area first.

"What happened to you?"

"You won't believe it. I was heading to Stilson's earlier and crashed right in front of Morgan Downer's house while she was in the front yard."

"No way. That must have been embarrassing," said Ricky.

"I fall hard, do a face plant right in her front yard, and then she literally patches up my knee—and—gave me a ride home."

"Dang, Pete. You should crash there more often," joked Little T.

"I wish I had that kind of a chance with her, but she's gone right after high school," I said.

"Pete. Nobody has a chance with her. Not even Parks or any of the popular guys," said Little T.

"Maybe she's a lesbo. You ever think of that?" said Ricky.

"Knock it off, Ricky," I said.

"I'm just sayin."

The ache in my knee had dulled, as if setting out on the trail itself was a balm. Hiking up this familiar path, one we'd trodden countless times in our youth, sometimes as knights hunting dragons, other times as soldiers hunting Commies, felt like a journey back in time to when imagination ruled. The air was warmer back here, but the ground beneath us was dry and solid. As we rounded a bend, hidden from the world, our old fort emerged from the foliage—still standing, untouched by time. Constructed from scavenged pallets and mismatched planks, it was a monument to our childhood ingenuity. We'd even used old roofing panels, deliberately leaving gaps in the slanted roof to let shards of daylight filter through.

Not far off, the mountain creek babbled like an old friend; its ceaseless flow, always a comfort to me, especially during the darker days right after my mom disappeared. I'd often escape here alone, letting the water's eternal journey serve as a reminder that even if I felt trapped, one day I, too, would find my flow and go with it. The creek was a natural antidepressant, a soothing soundtrack that whispered promises of movement, even when I felt most stuck. It was music to my ears right now.

We ducked down and entered the fort. Nothing had been touched and it was still dry.

"Oh, man! I forgot all about these. I'm taking one home," said Ricky as he grabbed a moldy old copy of a 1970's Playboy magazine that we found in the trash by the McDonalds one day after middle school. There was a whole stack — Playboy, Hustler — these magazines were really the first place the three of us learned anything about women. Little T.'s dad died when he was young and his mom raised him, his brother and sister all alone. Nobody talked to us about sex in a grown-up way, so we found out in our own way like most kids do.

"I can't look at those now that I've seen Amanda Breyer doin' it," said Little T.

"Yeah, seeing real milk jugs like that was awesome. I get a boner every time I think of her, if I'm being honest," said Ricky, then he looked at T. and shrugged his shoulders. "You gonna fire up that joint or what?"

"I've never smoked any pot before. Am I gonna be weirded out?" I said.

"Oh you're gonna like it. Makes the whole brain light up," said Ricky.

"For real. Everything gets silly. I like it better than drinking any day," said Little T. as he fished around in his jacket pocket and pulled out a small box of matches like the ones you get at a hotel.

He placed the joint between his lips and struck the match then lit it. He took the first hit, slow and deeply, then fell into a coughing fit while passing it to Ricky. Soon the fort was filled with lingering smoke. We were giggling about every little thing we talked about. It felt good to crack up with friends because nothing has been very funny the past few years. Ricky impersonated Principal Day and had me in tears. And I swear that the more Ricky got stoned, the straighter his lazy eye became. It was blowing my mind and when I pointed it out to Little T., he said I was crazy. We debated the subject while Ricky posed for us looking as straight ahead as he could.

It wasn't long before we leveled off and started doing what comes naturally to all Snydersvillians, which is talking serious crap about other people. When my dad was home, he used to tell me that the world's official rumor mill was based right in here Snydersville and lies, not railroad cars, was our towns biggest export. He was joking but now I knew it to be true in many ways because so much bad stuff is said about me all the time that's not true too.

"Did you guys hear about Tanya Smith?" said Ricky, leaning in all gossipy, as if anyone could hear us out here.

"No, what about her?" I said.

"She got pregnant with one of the police officers after getting pulled over for a speeding ticket. That's the rumor," said Ricky.

"For real?" said Little T.

"Which one? Sweet Chuck?" I said with a grin I could feel because it wouldn't go away.

"I heard it's Jenkins, the new guy," said Ricky. "Whoever it was had forced her to get an abortion when she told him."

"That girl is one year younger than us but ain't no way a cop is getting in trouble," said Little T.

"Hell no. Cops don't get in any trouble for anything they do around here," said Ricky.

"You know who the biggest drug dealer in town is, don't you?" added T.

"Who?" I said while taking another hit from the roach. It was so small now that my fingertips burned. I put it down on the dirt floor.

"The police chief, McMullen himself. He's the biggest coke head around. And he sells it in other towns. That's the rumor," said Little T., taking another pull on the joint while still talking. "And I know it's true because Travis Deenen got hooked on McMullen's coke and his parents had to send him to a detox place up in Buffalo."

"I thought Deenen was playing football up in Elmira," I said.

"Not anymore. His career is over. He's always in and out of rehab now," said Little T.

"Bastards," said Ricky.

"Hey...you guys got any idea about what you're going to do after we graduate?" I asked after a long pause where we must have been daydreaming about how messed up it was that Deenen wasted his talent. He was a local hero and then halfway through his senior year he—vanished. Drugs and druggies weren't everywhere you looked like drunks were, but it was starting to creep in, taking one or two futures at a time with it.

"I'm gonna go work with my uncle in his auto body shop. I already know what to do. I can fix any vehicle," said Little T.

"My dad wants me to work with him, but I got a helper position waiting up to Deer Kill Farm instead, if I want," said Ricky.

"Deer Kill? Doing what?" I asked.

"Shoveling crap, milking cows. Whatever. I know how to work a farm, Pete. You should know that. Why'd you ask?"

"Check this out. Mr. Stilson asked me to work for him full time and said I could hire one helper."

Ricky pointed at himself with both hands.

"I don't want to shovel crap or work with my dad, McCloskey. Hire me. We would rock that place."

"Let me see what he says. I didn't tell him yes yet."

We made our way to the creek where we skipped rocks without talking. We were all in a trance as the high came down and settled on us like a warm glow. Today started all wrong but ended up not so bad after all. We were trying to squeeze in some last fun, but after today it didn't feel so scary to be getting older. Eventually, the sun began its descent, casting long shadows across the water.

"Guess it's time to head back," Ricky said, breaking the silence.

"Yeah, my mom's gonna kill me if I'm late for dinner again," Little T. added.

We headed down the trail and they kept going once we got to my street, leaving me alone with my thoughts. I sat down on my crooked front steps and looked out at our weed-infested yard. It was an eyesore, a reflection of the neglect that had plagued our home for years. Then I remembered Morgan, her hands covered in soil as she tended to her garden, making something beautiful out of the earth. That sense of purpose washed over me again. It was a funny new feeling, so I got up, found some old gardening gloves and tools in the garage, and started pulling weeds while there was still daylight. I trimmed the overgrown bushes with dull shears and even managed to plant a few flower seeds I found in a forgotten corner of the garage. An hour passed, and by the time I was done, the front of the house looked transformed. It was still the same old place, but it felt a little less ugly, a little more like a home. I stood back and admired my work, dirt-streaked and sweaty but feeling... in control.

I understood that I could make things better if I got my hands dirty and tried. Change begins with the simplest of actions.

DIRTY LAUNDRY

I woke up early the next morning, my body still sore but my spirit lifted from yesterday's revelations. I knew what I had to do to initiate change around here. I filled a bucket with cold water from the tap, its icy chill almost numbing my fingers. I went into the living room first, but it was empty. Then I heard the faint sound of shallow snoring coming from the kitchen.

I walked in to find Troy sprawled out on the floor, an empty Jack Daniels bottle beside him.

"Here's goes nothin'," I muttered to myself. With a deep breath, I lifted the bucket high and dumped the water all over him, pouring it from head to toe, back and forth. Troy freaked out.

"What the—?!" He sprang up from the floor, banged his head on the table, drenched and furious, still half drunk.

"Pete, you dumb fucker!"

"How do you like cold showers, jerk!"

I bolted out of the kitchen, but Troy, despite his hangover, was surprisingly quick. He caught up to me in the living room, pushed my back so hard I fell into the couch, cans and bottles crashing away around me.

He got on my back, water dripping everywhere, and put me in a headlock.

"You've got some nerve. You wanna die today don't ya?"

I struggled to break free from his grip but managed to get the words out.

"If you want...more rent money from me...you've got to fix the power and the hot water heater. I ain't paying more for a place that's falling apart."

Troy dropped me, slapped my head hard and backed away from the couch, his eyes narrowing.

"You're serious?"

I rubbed my neck with both hands. "As a heart attack, Troy. I'm gonna move out, get my own place soon. But if you want me to stay and pay more, then you've got to hold up your end of the bargain."

Troy stepped back, massaging his temples as if trying to process a complicated equation. I know how desperate he was for money and likely why.

"Fine," he gave in, "I'll look into it but if you ever pull that shit again you better have a grave site picked out." He shivered and walked off to the bathroom to grab a nasty towel hung on the rack. I nodded, my heart still racing from the adrenaline.

"Good. Then we have a deal."

"Fuck off, Pete."

"Just fix what's broke."

I ran upstairs and took a fast cold shower washing myself better than I ever have before. I slicked my hair back and even used an old piece of metal to clean underneath my fingernails. I didn't know how gross I was until I got super clean. I stood in front of the broken mirror looking at my reflection split in half. I was seeing my life as it was—fractured. It hurt a little less now that I accepted what I knew to be true anyway.

The shame of what my father did and the embarrassment of how I was merely existing, had to end. I stared at myself for a moment, then left a few seconds later with a garbage bag of my dirty clothes and a pocketful of quarters.

Riding down the hill with my laundry over one shoulder and my other hand on the handlebar, I made it to the laundromat without crashing. The laundromat was at the bottom end of the street where most of the bars were. I chained up my bike. The only person with me was an old lady I would see around town all my life. She kept her white hair in a bun, her small pursed lips matted with very red lipstick that made her look judgmental and disappointed. I waved to her and when she didn't wave back, I looked closer and noticed that her heavily-lined eyes were closed while her laundry spun in the dryer right behind her head.

My clothes all fit in one machine. I added the detergent, paid with my quarters and pressed start. A row of faded plastic chairs lined the windows. I took a seat, propped my feet up on the heater and looked down the sunny street with all the bar signs washed out by the sunshine. They reflected and bounced light as if someone blotched them out.

Across the street a family came out of their small house. A mom and dad held a little girl by both hands. It was nothing unusual but made me sad because walking alone is all I know how to do in life, but I wanted nothing more than to hold someone's hand too. I didn't want the pain and sadness to come get me like it did Troy. I was going to do the opposite of him, make the opposite choices and never pick up drinking besides a little sip here, a little sip there with friends.

I hauled my laundry home and was shocked to

hear Troy banging around down in the basement. I put my garbage bag full of folded clothes up in my room, and ran down to see what was going on. The fridge door was wide open, the light was on and I heard it running again. I went out the back door and down into the basement to find Troy standing back chugging a can of beer, looking at an open fuse box. He looked over at me and shrugged with stupid look on his face.

"All it needed was a new fuse and there were some laying around down here," he said.

"There's gonna be hot water now too?"

Troy nodded his head in the direction of the water heater. I noticed the blue flame at the bottom.

"It's heating up now, I had to drain it first, it's gonna take a while but yeah, we'll have some hot water again."

I was in shock and knew what I had to do.

"I'll go get that extra rent money for you and be right back after I go the store."

Troy cracked another can of beer open. Looked at me all serious like.

"I'll be waiting."

I left him there among the old boxes of memories that littered the basement floor and rode my bike down to Acme feeling excited about taking hot showers at home. My heart felt lighter now, it was a strange feeling to me. Carrying a heavy heart is all you're left with once the bad things in life arrive, but a light heart with even a smidge of hope is like a helium filled balloon that makes everything easier to carry. I had never considered anyone's pain and drama but my own at that time because that's what surviving does to you. It makes you more of an animal than a human and animals run on pure instinct.

The grocery store parking lot was pretty empty. I pulled out a shopping cart and went up and down the aisles like an adult. There was a large bucket of peanut butter on sale that I picked up, one loaf of bread and a couple of oranges, some milk and cereal too. Then I remembered that if we have power in the kitchen and I can make toast, so I picked up some butter too.

Heading to the register I walked down the aisle that had toothpaste and deodorant and grabbed one of each before adding a bar of soap to my basket. I was going to live like a responsible young man from now on. Childhood was long gone and I couldn't let myself linger in the past anymore. It was up to me and only me and I knew it now.

Troy was waiting on the couch when I got back home. He was only ten beers deep at this time of day so bully brother was not who I encountered. He wanted that rent money badly. I paid him with cash that I got from my hiding spot and his eyes lit up when he saw the all the twenty-dollar bills.

"A deal is a deal," I said, hanging him the money. He ripped it from my hands and squeezed the cash hard.

"Thanks, Pete."

It had been years since I had a regular interaction with Troy that wasn't violent, hurtful or condescending. He looked at me staring at him, waiting for some insult out of habit.

"What?"

"That's it?" I said.

"We're good now until the rent is due again. Keep paying up and you won't have any more problems with me.

"Cool. Don't eat all my food."

He finished the beer, let out a loud burp, crumpled

the can and tossed it into a a pile of empty cans in the corner.

"Cool," I said and then went up to my room to take a hot shower at home for a change.

Later that night it was breezier than usual. I decided to follow Troy out and see where he was going now that he has extra cash. I suspected it was Amanda who he wanted the money for, and I was right.

Her street was quiet and dark, not a soul in sight when Troy turned down it. I hid my bike in the shrubs by the school again and waited. When he stumbled up onto the porch and started knocking on her door, I sprinted across the street and snuck into the shadowed area between houses.

Amanda stood up covered in a blanket and walked over to the door. She was shocked it was Troy and he was stone cold drunk. He came falling into her living room and leaned up against a wall while she retreated to other side of her apartment.

"What are you doing here, Troy? I have a restraining order."

Troy pulled out the cash — the money I paid him — out of his front pocket and waved it in the air.

"Look babe. I can afford to be with you now."

"Where did you get all that money?"

"Don't matter. It's for you, baby."

"Get out of my apartment, Troy."

"I need you Amanda. You're the last pretty thing left in this town," he said.

"You can't keep doing this to me and to yourself. It's not a healthy way to live."

"Oh and what you do is? You became the town slut!"

Amanda's body language stiffened. She had more

self respect than Troy and there was something painful in his words that she despised.

"Get out of my apartment right now or you're getting arrested. I mean it Troy McCloskey. You don't want to go to jail do you?"

Troy started crying and I felt sorry for him more than anything. He looked pathetic. He knew jail was where he'd be heading so he nodded silently, stuffed the cash in his pocket and backed out. She ran up and locked the door behind him then leaned on the door breathing heavy.

I froze in place and heard Troy's approaching footsteps as he walked past the house, towards the riverbank at the end of her street. Thank God, he didn't notice me. I ducked way down when Amanda came to the window and peeked out in the direction of the sidewalk. She was shaken up by Troy's visit and also looked worried about him, still caring in a weird way. She didn't look long and I got as far away from that house as possible. I ran to my bike, hopped on and rode towards the riverbank thinking about how she and Troy were once the king and queen of their senior prom. I remember it like it happened yesterday. Her parents dropped her off at our house back when it was nice. The two of them posed for pictures out back under the oak tree where my mom had a beautiful pepper garden. My dad let Troy drive his Ford Thunderbird to the dance. Life was normal back then. Life was life.

I saw Troy's figure silhouetted against the moonlight up on the riverbank, staggering but somehow purposeful. He looked like an animation the way shadows kept him in all black, but his outline was clear. My curiosity got the better of me, and I followed him again, keeping out of his line of sight under the maple trees down on the street level. A couple of blocks later, he came down from the riverbank and headed into town, straight for Lucky's.

I could have cut away and gone home, but I rode slow and veered across the street from Lucky's watching him from an old warehouse parking lot. The place was busy. Troy sat at the bar pounding down drinks like he was on a mission. Nobody talked to him. Observing this, a sadness washed over me. I leaned against my bike, unable to focus. The street with all the bars, their neon signs and glittering lights hazed out on me for a second. Tears welled up in my eyes because I knew back then that Troy was probably not going to make it. I had a premonition that rattled me that night.

Troy finally stumbled out, looking worse for wear, barely able to walk. I went up to him. "Need some help getting home?" I offered.

He squinted at me, then broke into a sloppy grin. "Hey I know you. You're Pete McCloskey, my little sack of shit brother!"

I knew better than to react when Troy was this drunk.

"Yep. That's me. Now let's get you home."

We started the uphill trek without saying a word, only the sounds of our feet crunching on gravel and broken glass. The houses we passed were like the people in them—worn down, paint peeling, and lights on low.

Snydersville at night sagged under the weight of its own despair sometimes, a place forgotten by time and luck. The whole way up our hill was pitch-black, the kind of darkness that feels almost heavy, pressing in from all sides. He took this walk alone every night and it mirrored the black hole I knew existed in his heart—a void that no amount of booze could ever fill. He stopped walking, bent over and puked his guts out all over the sidewalk and his shoes. When he stood straight again, he almost fell back while wiping vomit from his mouth.

"Let's sit down for a second," I said.

I helped him sit down on the curb beside me. We were high enough up the street to see the old train factory and Amanda's neighborhood from here. I noticed Troy gazing off in that direction while he rocked slightly in a drunken way.

"You ever think about Amanda?" I ventured, breaking the silence.

Troy stiffened, then his whole body seemed to straighten up.

"Every damn day, Pete. Every damn day."

We sat in silence for a long time. The cold concrete seeping through my jeans. We were both lost in our own broken lives but somehow closer for it in this one moment. Finally, Troy looked at me, his eyes bloodshot. The moonlight lit up his face, making him appear too white like all the blood was gone. He looked like a vampire.

"I messed up, Pete. I messed up real bad."

"Yeah," I said softly, "we both did."

Troy nodded, wiping his face with the back of his hand.

"Do you know what they call this area we live in?" I said, looking out across the valley.

"Hell?"

"No. The rust belt. You know why?"

Troy put both of his hands in his jacket pockets and shook his head no.

"Because the factories, like that one right there where dad used to work, have been closing down all over the place and the factories and the people are left to rust together. Nobody cares about us, so we have to care about ourselves is how I see it now."

He elbowed me. "How'd you get so smart?"

"I ain't smart. When I read the newspaper at work it gets me thinking. Remember how Dad used to say that railroad track steel runs through your spine back when you were playing football. Remember that?"

Troy chuckled; a sound devoid of any real joy. "Yeah, but steel rusts."

"Exactly," I said, seizing the moment. "You know what makes steel rust?"

"I remember that from metal shop...water and oxygen...salt in the water, and impurities in the steel work together and the steel corrodes from the inside out," said Troy, as he looked at me, puzzled but intrigued. "So, what's your point?"

"My point is, maybe we are all a bit like that steel. We've got these elements—our past, our mistakes, our town's decline, our bad habits—that are making us corrode. We're rusting, Troy, from the inside out. But rust can be stopped and treated if you catch it in time. I know that from taking care of my bike."

For a moment, Troy pondered my theory, his eyes narrowing as he looked down the street, where the old railroad factory stood on the opposite side of the riverbank rusting—a giant relic of better times.

"So, you think we can stop the rust? How's that supposed to happen?" he finally asked.

"By not letting the elements around us get into our weaknesses. We can't change the oxygen or the salt, but maybe we can remove some of the impurities, make the steel a bit more resistant. That's why I don't want to drink, Troy."

Troy sighed, his shoulders slumping. "Maybe

you're right, I dunno. Maybe it's time to scrub off some of that rust, I really don't know how anymore, Pete."

As we sat there, the weight of our conversation hanging in the air, I couldn't help but feel that we'd found a sliver of truth amid the corrosion between us. Then, with a newfound resolve, we stood up. Side by side, we continued our walk up the hill, each step a tiny rebellion against the gravity that sought to pull us back down.

THE SON ALSO RISES

Dad strolled into the visitation room, free of handcuffs this time. He looked more at ease, as if my newfound sense of purpose had unshackled him too. He looked at me funny, noticing my cleaned-up appearance, a departure from my usual disheveled look.

"Hey kiddo. You're looking sharp. I've been thinking about you."

"Where's the handcuffs?"

"No more. They moved me to a lower security wing for model prisoners. I've been good and it looks like you've been getting busy livin'."

"Yessir. And I have a bruise to prove it and stories to tell." I hiked up my left pant leg up so he could see the wound that was still healing.

"How'd you end up with that?"

"Crashed my bike looking at a pretty girl."

He smiled big and it made me feel good.

"Now that sounds more like the son of Billy McCloskey. Chasing tail is what I was good at when I was your age, but you're not supposed to literally fall for one, Pete."

"I know that now, but it worked in my favor because she's the one who patched me up and I got to know her better. Oh, and I started hanging out again with my friends too. Tried some new things."

"Women like to fix a man, Pete. If she's helping you in any way, she likes you. Tell me all about what you and your friends got into."

"Do you remember Ricky Larson, Little Tyrone? We drank some vodka, spied on some chicks and almost got in a brawl all in one night. It was pretty wild."

"I said try one beer, just for kicks. Vodka is hard liquor. Were you drunk?"

"Only buzzed because I had a little. I'll get drunk later. Buzzed is good enough, right?"

"Fine. Buzzed is fine. That's what most people are looking for to take the edge off...but tell me more about this girl who helped you."

"She's...beautiful, Dad."

"What's her name?"

"Morgan."

"That's a pretty name. Rolls off the lips. What's she like?"

"She's cool, she's smart, she's actually going places and nothing bothers her but she's leaving town when school is out so I don't know if it will go anywhere long term."

The more I told him about my exploits, the more alive and animated he became. I kept stretching the truth by telling him what I wanted to happen, not what really happened.

"It's been so long, Pete, I can hardly remember what a woman is like. The touch of her hair, the smell of her skin. The taste of her lips. Did you kiss her yet?"

"Not yet. We started being friends recently."

He looked up for a moment, recalling in his mind the old days of his own youth that he was now reliving through me. "The day you really experience your first woman is the day your life changes forever."

"What do you mean?"

"Nothing will be the same again after that. The whole world, everything around you is going to be different. Life is all perception and after you've been to that place where life begins...everything gets easier, more in your control. It's hard to explain."

"Are you talking about doing it?"

"Yes. It's the most pleasant experience there is and the first time is always the best. Only catch is: you can only do it once so choose wisely and don't get anyone pregnant or your whole life will be put on pause."

I sat there knowing it was never gonna happen. I held Morgan in too high of a regard to think of her like that. She was too important for me objectify, even in my mind.

"Think you'll be ready to cross that road when the moment hits?" he said.

"Probably not with this girl. I'm not even positive she'll remember me after graduation. How do people know when they're ready?"

"You'll know. You'll both know, whoever it is. It creeps up on you and your girl until you can't fight the feeling anymore. It's nature, Pete. Don't fight it is all I'm saying."

That day he gave me my first birds and bees talk in his own twisted way from behind bars. The whole way back to Snydersville I fantasized about getting close to Morgan but not in the way my dad was thinking. I played along, wanting to sound cool for him, but I admired Morgan and more than anything wanted to be closer to her because of how she made me feel. She was going places and had that energy about her and it rubbed off. Even though I couldn't go with her, I wished that I could. I rode straight to Stilson's and let him know about my plans.

"I didn't expect to see you on your day off, Pete."

"Well, I've thought it through and came to tell you that although I'm a young man with many options piling up, I accept your offer for a full-time job after I graduate."

Mr. Stilson looked at me, nodding in an approving way.

"That's what I wanted to hear. That's great news. You'll start the new schedule right after school ends. I'll put an ad in the paper to find you an assistant."

"I might know exactly the right person."

"Send him in to see me and I'll interview whoever you suggest."

"OK. One last thing. I was wondering...could I get a small advance on my paycheck this week? I need a couple of things around the house, making some changes. It's real important."

"How much do you need?"

"Two hundred bucks."

Mr. Stilson only looked at me over the top of his glasses when he was not buying what I said. That was the look he gave me.

"I'd love to Pete, but how do I know you're not going to change your mind about the job over the next few weeks?"

"Because I won't. I always keep my word."

"Your word is good, but I don't know. I have to think about it a little. Ask me again tomorrow when you come in."

"Alright sounds good," I said, then slapped the counter and pointed at him with both hands like a cowboy with dual finger pistols, before heading out.

"Don't forget to send your friend in to see me," he said.

Spring was coming in fast, and the day got nicer in an instant. I rode my bike into town feeling good because I had something stable and accepted that it was for me. Stability makes all things easier to understand and I was starting to know myself more than ever.

I rode past my school and the summer baseball league was out on the field doing weekend practice. More people were out and about and for a moment I got a glimpse of normal life where time is filled with activities and goals instead of looking backwards at bitter memories and pain too loud to ignore. Maybe normal life was always happening around me and I was too blind to see it.

I rolled into downtown where Morgan's car was parked in front of the barber shop that doubled as the bus station. The hazard lights were flashing and the car was running but nobody was in it. As I reached the front of the store Morgan came out and nearly walked right into me she while was reading a small pamphlet.

"Oh, hi Morgan."

She looked up as I stopped my bike and waited for her to cross my path.

"Hey Pete. You look different. What did you do?"

"I invested in a comb and some gel."

"You look good showing your face. How's the knee feeling?"

"Nothing but a scar now thanks to you."

"That's what all pain becomes eventually—a scar, healed over and stronger than before."

Morgan was profoundly smart and that made her even more beautiful. I smiled awkwardly while my brain melted thinking about what she had said. I wasn't feeling better about my life because pain didn't exist, I felt better because a scar was forming now.

She had a folded Greyhound schedule in her hand.

"What do you got there? You don't get haircuts at the barber shop."

"This? It's the bus schedule. My mom needs the car when I'm away at school and I won't need one where I'm going."

"Where are you going?"

"NYU School of Medicine. I'm so excited to begin. I can't wait."

"Down in New York City? Aren't you scared about living in that place?"

"No Pete. I fear not living. That's what keeps me moving."

I stiffened up, adopting a fearless take that matched her own confidence.

"Me too. It's popular around here, not living, but I am starting to see through it now, I really am. I'm happy for you. It's gonna be awesome."

"Thanks Pete. Well...I gotta get back home. See ya in school?"

"I'll be there."

I watched her get in the car and drive off, then shimmied over to the window to check out the bus schedule. There was one bus that left for NYC every Monday, Wednesday and Friday. An old man was getting his hair cut by the barber, who stopped the buzzer and looked at me over the top of his bifocals. I pulled back from the window and went home, cutting through downtown and past the bars.

. . .

Around dusk I left home and rode down the hill and across town to the Southside Mobile Trailer Park. It was tucked behind a thick wall of trees beyond the railroad tracks. If anyplace in Snydersville really was the wrong side of the tracks, this was it. The paved road changed into dirt as you enter the property. Trailers were spaced apart at angles. I saw a white van with Larson's Septic Maintenance Services painted on the side, hopped off my bike and laid it on the ground. When I looked up, Ricky's dad came from around the side of the truck with his tools in hand. He had a big scar across his cheek that healed over thick. It made him look mean but he was nicer than almost about anyone in town.

"Hey, Pete. What brings you over?"

"I'm looking for Ricky. Is he home?"

"He's inside. Go on in."

"Thanks, Mr. Larson."

When you step into Ricky's trailer home the first you see is a giant velvet picture of Jesus Christ, framed and on display above the couch. Ricky was laying down watching TV beneath it. He saw me come in and sat up, surprised.

"Hey man, what are you up to?" I asked.

"Nothin' much. What are you doing over here?" Said Ricky.

"I didn't feel like laying around the house waiting for Monday."

"Nice. I'm game. What do you wanna do?"

"Goof off. Anything. We gotta do more, ya know?" I said, with an antsy energy that came from self-imposed pent-up reclusiveness.

"My dad doesn't want me hanging out all night anymore. I got in trouble last time."

"Hanging out ain't against the law," I said.

Mr. Larson came inside with more tools in his hands, goes to the sink and starts washing them off.

"Dad, can I go hang out with Pete for a little bit?"

"You can hang out around here but no more all nighters. Don't head into downtown where there's nothing but drunks at this hour."

"Dad, we're gonna walk the tracks and talk about hot girls."

"Go ahead. But don't make me come find you if you're not back before too late."

"Don't worry Mr. Larson, we ain't interested in trouble," I said.

"We're just gonna skip some rocks," said Ricky.

Ricky slid into his sneakers, threw on a baseball hat and together we walked through the trailer park and cut through the trails that connect to the train tracks. It was a full moon night and the reflection made the tracks appear to shine like beams of light stretching into the darkness.

"What did your dad mean about getting into trouble again?"

"Man. You don't even know...I used to shoplift everything. Candy, books, toys, tools, you name it. One night I got caught and the cops brought me home. They found all my stolen stuff in my bedroom and and took it back and warned me and my dad that I'd be heading to juvie hall if I don't stop. Now I don't have jack shit."

"Me neither."

"At least we got the tracks. They go somewhere," said Ricky.

"You ever think about hitching a ride when a train is passing and you just keep on riding?"

Ricky looked at me then picked up a rock and

skipped it down one of the rails. He had a good side arm throw that made dinging noises as it stayed the course.

"Sometimes. But then I chicken out because I don't like the idea of hitching my way back. There're too many weirdos around for that," he said.

"Hey, why'd the cops bring you home in the first place?"

"Remember the big article in the newspaper about all the missing stop signs around town? And everyone was talking about it like some big thing because it's illegal to steal traffic signs?" he said.

"Yeah."

"That was me. I got caught in the act but since I was a minor, they drove me home instead of to jail and that's when the found all my other stuff."

"All you got was a warning. You're so lucky."

"I got probation all summer long last year and it sucked."

We walked in silence for a while, picking up and skipping rocks. My aim was bad compared to Ricky's, but I got a couple to skate down the line.

"Can I ask you something personal, Pete?"

"Anything, man."

"What happened to your mom? I've never seen her or hear you say anything about her but I have this weird memory of her picking you up in kindergarten."

"She's dead as far as I know. That's why I never talk about her."

"You don't even know if she's alive?"

"Nope."

"You ever gonna try and find out?"

"Probably not. When the thing with my dad happened, she left me and Troy and it's been a living Hell ever since. More than anyone, I blame her for how bad it got at home."

"But that's your mom. You ever think about trying to find her…if she's still alive?"

"I used to. I dreamed that someday she'd come back and get me and then take me to a nice house in a nice town and let me live with her there."

"That sucks, man. Cancer took my mom and I think about her every day. I know my dad does too."

"You're lucky. At least you knew her."

"You ever wonder where you're gonna be five years from now?" he asked.

"All the time and I hate it because I always see myself exactly the same as I am now, and I really don't want to exist like this for the rest of my life. That's why I'm trying to change."

Ricky stopped walking and looked at me. "In my dreams I never change either. I'm always stuck in-between, skipping rocks down the tracks for the rest of my life."

"It sucks to have life stretching out before us but we can't even get out of our own backyards," I said.

"True."

A large raccoon scurried across the tracks and scared us both. We picked up rocks and zinged them towards it as it ran away into the bushes on the other side.

"Damn they're quick," said Ricky.

"I think you hit its tail at least once because I saw it jump."

Ricky tugged at my shirt, his voice barely above a whisper, "You see that? Someone's down there."

We stepped off the tracks, melting into the shadows beneath the trees. Straining our ears, we caught the murmur of a distant voice. Moments later, a tall figure emerged from the opposite side of the tracks where the raccoon ran, a long rifle slung over his shoulder. He was followed by two more men, also armed with rifles. They paused, standing directly in front of where we were hidden. One of their radios crackled to life, confirming they were from the Sheriff's department and were out searching for someone.

Gnats buzzed around our necks and arms, but we dared not move, not even to swat them away. It felt like an eternity before the officers finally moved on, their boots crunching gravel as they walked further down the tracks spread apart. The moment they were out of sight, we bolted, sprinting through the trails back to Ricky's trailer.

As we reached the safety of his front steps, a helicopter roared by overhead, its searchlight sweeping the area like a giant, unblinking eye. Gasping to catch our breath, we laid back on the steps when the door swung wide open. Mr. Larson appeared, his face stern. "Get inside, now," he ordered. I glanced back to see the helicopter's searchlight illuminating the railroad tracks, tracing the path the officers had taken. The tension hung thick in the air, a reminder that something far more serious was unfolding around us.

"You boys made it back just in time."

"What's going on, Dad?" said Ricky.

The TV news was on and the story was a prison break up at Mapleton where my dad was in jail. My heart sunk as the news showed a map of the area where they think the escaped prisoner was suspected of hiding out.

"Mr. Larson did they say who escaped?" I asked.

"A fella named Danny Huntly. They said he's been missing for about three hours now and he probably came down to Snydersville area to hop a freight train."

"You OK, Pete?" said Ricky.

"I am now."

"It's been a long time since they've had a breakout at Mapelton," said Mr. Larson.

"One year and fifteen days to be exact. I hate when it happens. It means my life is going to really suck tomorrow. Maybe I won't even go to school."

"You gotta stay here for a bit. Wanna play cards?"

"Sure."

We sat at the small kitchen table and Ricky dealt out a couple of hands of five-card poker while Mr. Larson sat in the living room watching the news. I kept my attention on it too. The search went on and it was getting late and there was school tomorrow, probably in a lock-down mode.

"Pete, I'll give you a ride home. It's late, and I don't want you biking alone, especially with whatever's going on out there."

"Thanks, Mr. Larson," I said, relieved.

We got into his old pickup, the engine rumbling to life as he turned the key. Ricky sat in the back, leaning in between us. As we drove, Mr. Larson glanced over at me. "You know, I knew your father back in the day. He was always a good guy, had a lot of school spirit."

I looked out the window, contemplating his words. "Yeah, he's got spirit, alright. It's not always the kind that helps you out."

Mr. Larson chuckled. "Well, nobody's perfect. But I see the same good nature in you, Pete. It's easy to lose your cool, especially when life throws its weight at you. Being disciplined is a lot harder than losing your cool, but we all make mistakes, Pete. Everyone."

I nodded, absorbing his words. They hit close to home. My dad's mistake was costing me every day but maybe it didn't need to. We pulled up to my house, and Mr. Larson put the truck in park. "You take care now, Pete. And think about what I said, alright?"

"I will, Mr. Larson. Thanks for the ride and the advice."

"Anytime, kid."

"See ya tomorrow, Ricky."

Ricky said nothing. He had fallen asleep in the leaning position.

I got out of the truck and watched as they drove down the hill, taillights fading into the distance. I stood there for a moment, reflecting on his words that I knew so well were true. Being disciplined is way harder than losing your cool. I thought about my dad, Troy, my friends, and all the chaos that defined my life. I realized that I had a choice in how I reacted to it all. And maybe I could find the discipline within me to make the right choices going forward.

THE SINS OF THE FATHER

Nobody knows what it's like being me on the days following a prison break. Nobody except Troy, but he can handle his business and people know not to pick a fight with him. It was always my fault and my problem because people need someone to blame when they feel afraid. I knew it and the adults knew it too but even then, they acted strange towards me when it happened.

I got to school on time and as I chained my bike to the rack, I overheard Principal Day and Mr. Logan talking outside the front door, a little on edge compared to other days.

"It's getting bad around here with these breakouts. With convicts in your back yard, who can sleep well at night?" said Principal Day.

"The negligence at Mapleton is an embarrassment to the whole region. Somebody needs to get fired. Did you hear where they finally caught him?" said Mr. Logan.

"Over by the tracks in North Snydersville. He was going to hop a freight train to the Canadian border," said Day, disgusted.

"I'm glad it was over fast, unlike the last time when we were on edge for weeks," said Mr. Logan.

"Me too," I chimed in as I headed into school. Ricky caught up to me and saluted Principal Day.

"Private Larson reporting for wall and personal hygiene duty!" said Ricky.

"It's nice to see you on time, Pete," said Principal Day.

"I couldn't sleep last night. Was too scared," I said, referring to his conversation with Mr. Logan.

Ricky put his arm around me when we walked through the double doors.

"If anyone says anything about last night's breakout to you, remember that this prison sentence right here in Sny High here ends soon and you won't ever have to see any of these assholes again."

"Last time there was a breakout we got a brick through our window," I reminded him.

"Forget yesterday, man. Get through today and nobody will be talking about it by next week. We've got long boring lives ahead of us, ya know?" He said with his trademark half-crazy smile.

We parted ways as he went into the main office and the rest of us dashed to our classrooms before the final bell rang.

"Hey McCloskey, I heard your dad tried to pay you a visit this weekend. Had the whole town on lockdown. Tell him to stay where he belongs, will ya?" Chad sneered.

"Yeah, McCloskey, why don't you stand up and apologize for ruining everyone's Sunday night?" Will chimed in, reveling in my humiliation. But I was done being their punching bag, done being the target of their bullying. My father's mistakes weren't mine to bear.

I slowly pushed back my chair with a screech that echoed in the classroom, stood up, and locked eyes with Chad. My heart was pounding so hard I could hear it in my ears. I must've looked unhinged because Chad hesitated, suddenly unsure of picking on me.

"Sit down, McCloskey. Apologize, and I promise I won't mess with your stuff anymore," Chad said, grinning like he'd already won.

I felt a surge of adrenaline and before I knew it, I was lunging at Chad, leaving him no time to react. My fists connected with his face, one punch after another. He was helpless and crumpled to the floor, blood spattering from his nose. Desks toppled over, papers flew, and the room erupted into chaos as I grabbed Chad by the collar and wailed on him with all of my might. Students scrambled away, clearing a circle around us. I left Chad on the floor, turned to Will, my fists clenched. He was backed into a corner, his eyes wide with fear.

"You want some too? I'll end both of you right now! Is that what you want?"

"Calm down, Pete, it was a joke," Will stammered.

"You two are the joke. And you're not funny," I spat back.

Mr. Logan bear-hugged me, pulling me back with a powerful grip. I was still seething, my eyes locked onto Chad as I was pulled from the classroom.

"Don't you ever call me names again, or you'll regret it! Do you hear me? Do you?!"

Mr. Logan dragged me out of the room, pinning me against the hallway wall like I was the instigator. Mrs. Shelmire burst out of her classroom across the hall, alarmed by the commotion. Students peeked out of classrooms all the way down the hall.

"Get Chad to the nurse, now!" Mr. Logan barked.

Chad stumbled out, clutching a wad of bloody paper towels to his nose, and sprinted down the hall with Mrs. Shelmire. Seeing him run away like that—broken, afraid—gave me a sense of triumph I'd never felt before. It dawned on me: I was stronger than most people here, not in muscle but in mettle. I'd been the target for so long that I'd built up an immunity. Now, I was willing to fight back and win and my tormentors folded like a wet noodle.

"Let's go," Mr. Logan said, still gripping my arm.

"Where?"

"The principal's office. You've crossed a line, Pete. You're finished here."

"I was defending myself."

"Save it for Principal Day. I don't want to hear it."

As we walked down the hall, my steps were heavy, but my spirit was lighter. I'd stood up for myself, and in doing so, I'd shattered the chains that had held me down for so long inside the walls of this building.

It wasn't my first time witnessing a fight at school, but it was the first time I'd ever thrown the punches that wrecked someone else. And with my dad's reputation looming over me like a dark cloud, especially after last night, I felt the weight of adult eyes on me, tinged with a fear I hadn't sensed before. Like they knew it was only was matter of time for me to turn all the way bad. My vision blurred with angry tears, not from the adrenaline rush alone, but from the crushing vice grip of my situation. Just when I was starting to see a glimmer of light at the end of the high school tunnel, I'd snapped. I'd let myself down.

As we walked past a classroom, I caught Morgan's eye. She was sitting at a desk near the door, and when she looked up and our eyes met, her expression shifted from curiosity to concern. That's when anger turned to sadness. I was massively disappointed in myself.

By the time we reached the office, tears and snot smeared across my face. The secretary hastily slid a box of tissues across the counter toward me. Ricky, who was already there, turned around and looked up, his eyes widening at the sight of me.

"Damn, Pete. What happened?" Ricky whispered.

I couldn't muster a word, just shook my head, my throat choked up with emotion.

Principal Day appeared in his doorway, surveyed the scene, and beckoned Mr. Logan inside. Their conversation was muffled but audible. "Pete attacked Chad Parks," Mr. Logan was saying. "Looks like Chad's nose is broken, he's on his way to the hospital. It's bad. He could have killed him."

I clenched my fists, my nails digging into my palms. They were all afraid of me, not because of who I was, but because of who my father had been. His past was my life sentence in this town, and I resented them all for it.

I felt a gentle touch on my arm. It was Morgan, holding out a small cup of water for me. "You okay, Pete?" she asked, her eyes searching mine. I took the cup, our fingers briefly touching. "I'm fine," I managed to say, gulping down the water. "Thank you."

Principal Day's voice cut through the moment. "Pete, in my office. Now."

I walked in, my head hung low, hands deep in my pockets and collapsed into the chair. He handed me a box of tissues, and we sat in silence as I wiped my face clean.

"So, want to tell me what made you snap?" he finally asked.

"I did not snap. I refuse to take it anymore, all the picking and harassment," I said, my voice tinged with desperation. "I'm sick of being a punching bag."

Principal Day sighed. "Chad's being dealt with. But you, Pete, you're instantly suspended for this. Two weeks."

I felt like I'd been slapped. "So I'm the one being punished? Again?"

"It's school policy, Pete. You've been involved in too many disruptions and violence is the red line. You sent him to the hospital, Pete."

I was stunned, speechless. School was over in three weeks. How could he do this to me when I have been trying so hard to make it to the end. I knew the answer, which was that he didn't care about anyone and wanted the problem gone. "Can I at least have lunch before I go? It's the only hot meal I'll eat today."

"Yes, you may. And then you're to leave and not return for two weeks. It's up to you to get your assignments from your teachers and hand them in on time or you will not be getting that diploma. You can go clear out your locker now and the come back here and face the opposite wall until lunch."

I nodded, accepting my fate, stood up, my body feeling heavy, and walked out of the office. I whispered a quick update to Ricky and then trudged down the hallway, my shoulders slumped, my thoughts a jumbled mess. And when I thought I was truly alone, Morgan appeared beside me, her pace matching mine.

"Hey," Morgan says, breaking into my cloud of thoughts. I stop, turning to face her.

"You always catch me at my worst," I admit, my voice tinged with embarrassment.

"I hope Principal Day wasn't too harsh on you," she says, her eyes searching mine.

"He's always a jerk to me, always has been," I sigh, feeling the weight of the day's events.

Morgan's eyes narrow, her concern palpable. "But are you going to be okay?"

I shake my head, defeated. "I don't know. I got suspended for the rest of the year. Finishing all the assignments I'm behind in is going to be impossible. Graduation might be off the table now. How can he do that me?"

"I'm really sorry. I know you've been working hard to turn things around. What's your next move?" she pressed, her eyes never leaving mine.

"I guess I'm gonna work full-time at Stilson's for the rest of my life and put this whole high school nightmare behind me. My real life starts when this place is in my rearview mirror, but I really wanted to graduate."

Morgan pauses, her eyes thoughtful. "How about we meet up later tonight? Texas Cafe? I have an idea."

I'm stunned. I even turn around to see if she's talking to someone behind me. "Wait, you want to go on a date with me? The guy who just got suspended?"

Her smile was warm, almost radiant. "It's not a date, it's a mission. I can help you study, get your assignments sorted. We can make a plan to ensure you still graduate. How does seven o'clock sound?"

I'm floored, one door closes and another one opens. "Seven o'clock works. I'll be there."

"Great," she says, her eyes twinkling. "And Pete, don't let today get to you. School is almost finished, you're almost free."

"Ok. Only for you. I won't let it get to me," I assure her, but inside, I'm already feeling lighter.

Morgan starts to walk away but then turns back. "We're going to make this happen, Pete. You're going to walk across that stage and get your diploma, and I'm going to help you do it."

Her conviction was so strong, it's almost tangible. "Why are you doing this?" I have to ask. "Why go to all this trouble for me?"

"Because everyone deserves a chance, Pete. And you're not the only one who wants to see you succeed. See you at seven."

As she walked away, I was left standing there, amazed not only by her kindness, but by her unwavering belief in me. Maybe I can turn things around. And with Morgan on my side, the odds feel a whole lot better.

I cleared out my locker which didn't have much in it anyway and then went classroom to classroom and collected my final assignments and worksheets before heading back to the front office until lunch time.

I sat at a table with Ricky and Little T., our lunch spread out before us. Little T. got so engrossed in his food that he hardly ever looks up while talking.

"You really smashed Chad up, huh?" Ricky remarked, studying my face.

I shrug, still processing it all. "I guess."

"I didn't know you had it in you. I figured you did, just didn't know for sure," said Little T.

"I'm suspended because of it. I have to leave the building after lunch." I pause for a moment, gazing out the window, reflecting on my newfound freedom.

"What? For real? Just like that? You're done with this place?" said Little T.

"Just like that. Day suspended me and said that I could only graduate if I currently had a passing average and can make up the work I'll be missing." I explained, the disappointment weighing on me because I knew I would not graduate now unless Morgan could work a miracle.

"Damn, Pete. You get all the lucky breaks, you know that?" Ricky remarked, half-jokingly.

I don't find it amusing. Instead, I glanced around the room, feeling the weight of four wasted years of perpetual struggle to fit in, be present and participate in my own life while at home it was a constant struggle to just be. Suddenly, Chad's voice cuts through our conversation. He was back from the hospital and looked awful.

"Hey McCloskey," Chad's voice echoes, grabbing everyone's attention. He stands at the end of the lunch line, holding a tray covered in food. His bandaged nose made him appear less menacing.

"What do you want?" I respond, turning to face him.

"I wanna talk to you, call a truce."

Ricky glances at me, then back at Chad, concern etched on his face. "Think he means it?"

I rise from my seat and walk toward Chad, Ricky cautiously trailing behind.

"I wanna talk alone," Chad asserts, ordering Ricky to stay back.

Ricky complies, crouching on a nearby bench seat, ready to intervene if needed. He comically flexes his arm in Chad's direction, trying to lighten the tension.

As I stand facing Chad, it's the first time I get a clear look at him. The sight of his purple and swollen face confirms that he's been on the receiving end of a beating, and it doesn't feel good. I should know, but I also know it don't feel good to give one either.

"What do you want from me? Spit it out," I said.

Chad takes a moment, his aggressive demeanor softening. "I'm sorry, man. I wanna call a truce. I'm sorry about all the jokes and stuff."

"We were never at war, Chad. You're the one who didn't like me."

"I don't want any more trouble between us then. How's that?"

Chad seemed sincere. Considering his words, I knew that harboring grudges and animosity serves no purpose anymore and I didn't want to hold one against him either.

"That's fine by me. I never wanted any trouble in the first place."

"Why'd he do it?" Chad asks, and it catches me off guard.

"Why'd who do what?"

Chad's voice reveals a mix of curiosity, uncertainty and fear.

"Why did your dad kill that man?"

I looked Chad in the eyes for a long moment and without blinking,"Because he didn't like him. Rage runs in my family. I choose to keep it bottled up all these years."

He got more serious and probed further. "Would you have killed me if the teacher didn't pull you off?"

I pause for a moment, considering his question.

"Most likely."

I held his frightened gaze a little longer before turning away, making my way back to where Ricky is waiting. Sitting down, I start to eat. Ricky can't contain his curiosity.

"What was that all about?"

"He suddenly wants to be cool now."

"Punk," Ricky scoffs. "Punk who got thumped."

We continued our meal, contemplating the strange turn of events and the newfound truce between Chad and me and how all things come to an end, usually when they are faced without fear and with action.

When lunch was done, Ricky got an idea that I didn't think was good, but he did it anyway.

SUSPENDED LIFE

Ricky was galvanized by my situation and choose to share in my suspension as a form of solidarity even though it was gonna cost him big time. We strode out of the front doors together right after lunch, our steps defiant.

Principal Day, seeing the rebellion, burst out of his office to intercept us. We were already halfway down the sidewalk by the time he made it to the door.

"If you leave with him, Ricky, consider yourself uninvited back to this school. You won't graduate!" Principal Day's voice carried a tone of passive-aggressive concern that was hard to miss.

Ricky paused, turning to look back at him. "I appreciate the sentiment, Shelly, but honestly, I'll be too preoccupied enjoying my life to even care!"

I couldn't help but laugh when Ricky called Principal Day by his first name. It was a well-known fact that he despised being called 'Shelly,' a short form of his actual name, Sheldon. It was like poking a bear with a stick.

"You'll both end up in prison. Mark my words!" he yelled, retreating into the building. I wish I had known back then that his concern was never genuine; it was all about maintaining his school's reputation, which meant managing the 'problem kids' like Ricky and me and then sliding us out the door at the end. And let's be honest, the school system was terrible at best. Most adults in Snydersville did the bare minimum while expecting us kids to give 150%, knowing full well we couldn't afford to meet those expectations. That kind of pressure often led us to reject even the valuable lessons some tried to impart.

"So, what's the plan now that we're officially free men?" Ricky asked, his eyes gleaming, a mix of excitement and disbelief. We stood just off school property, marveling at the realization that there was no physical fence holding us back. The only barriers were those of time and age, and we were teetering on the edge of adulthood.

"How about we go see Mr. Stilson about that job?" I suggested.

"Hell yeah," Ricky agreed, his face lighting up. "When I get home, I can tell my dad I got hired. That should cushion the blow about the whole school thing."

"Does he know about your in-school suspension for the past two weeks?"

"He knows, and he won't give a damn that I walked out, as long as I've got a job lined up. He's always said I don't need a diploma to work with him. But between you and me, I have zero interest in doing that."

"So, what's been keeping you in school all this time?" I asked, genuinely puzzled.

"Free lunch," he said, grinning.

I chuckled. "Same here, man. I'm gonna miss those taco salads."

My bike had pegs on the back wheels. Ricky hopped on, and we began our journey to Stilson's, each of us contemplating the gravity of the choice we'd made. It was weird to know that I got suspended for beating up Chad and that I had a date with Morgan later on the same night. Taking an action, even a violent one, opens the world up. It's hard to understand until life makes you know it.

We rolled into Stilson's as he was ringing up a customer at the counter. Since I didn't have work until later I parked my bike in front. He didn't notice us yet, but when the bell jingled as Ricky and I casually strolled into the store he looked surprised to see me.

"Aren't you supposed to be in school?" asked Stilson.

"I just got suspended for the next two weeks."

"School's almost over, in what, three weeks? What happened this time?"

"He got sick of Chad Parks picking on him about his dad and he sent Chad in the hospital with a broken nose," said Ricky, proud of my accomplishment.

"Who are you?" said Stilson.

"Oh, my bad. I'm Ricky Larson. Pete mentioned you might have a job for me."

"Did you both get suspended?"

"No, he decided to come with me," I said.

"Yeah, I wasn't gonna graduate so I decided to move on with my life starting today," said Ricky.

"And you want to work here, with Pete?"

"Yessir," said Ricky.

"Ricky's good people he just didn't do good in school like me. We aren't all cut out for it."

"Your old man owns Larson Septic Maintenance?"

"Yessir," said Ricky.

"I graduated with him. He's a good man."

"My dad graduated?"

"Yep."

"I did not know that," said Ricky.

Stilson glanced over at me doing a pre-work check on the wine and beer stocks while they talked some more. "Pete is going to be taking my place and he knows how to run the store like I'm still here. You'd have to take over his job full time, which is noon to closing hour, five days a week."

"All that time, work, work, work? No breaks?" asked Ricky.

"There's breaks and downtime. You'll be keeping the store stocked and clean, help load customers cars up...stuff like that," said Stilson.

Ricky looked at me. I nodded to him like "you got this, easily."

He looked back at Stilson, who was waiting with a funny grin, getting a kick out of Ricky's way of talking.

"I can do it and you can trust me. Ask Pete. I will be here on time every day," said Ricky.

"I do trust Pete so I'll go ahead and trust you too. Since you boys have a bunch of newfound free time how about you both start the day after tomorrow, that way I can get a head start on my weekend camping trip."

I looked at Ricky, he shrugged and nodded yes.

"Sounds like a plan, Mr. Stilson. I'll report for work at 9am and Ricky will be here at noon." We looked at each other and slapped five like quitting school early was never done before. We invented it and now we were adults.

"I'll be up at my Loon Lake cottage for the weekend with my wife and granddaughters. Not too far if you need me but it'll be a good trial run and it should be pretty busy too."

The door jingled and I turned around to see the

two guys who were looking for Troy a couple of weeks ago. The bigger one had a shiner, not fresh but still painful looking. He gave me the death stare, but because Stilson was behind the counter they acted cool and shopped for beer. Ricky and I left together. Outside there was a car waiting with two more goons in it I have not seen before.

"Can you drop me closer to my house?" said Ricky, as I peered through the window inside, the two goons were staring back at us, talking to each other. The one with the black eye was Randall Fitz and he locked eyes with me. A shiver ran down my spine; something was off.

"Absolutely, let's go," I said, my voice tinged with urgency.

We hadn't gone far down the road when the old, rusted Chevy began to tail us, matching our speed. Randall, shiner big and fresh, leaned out the window, a sneer on his face, he had a chip on his shoulder.

"Where's Troy? Got some buddies who'd love to have a chat with him."

"It looks like you already talked to Troy. Tell your buddies Troy said they can find him on his front lawn. He's ready to give out more shiners," I retorted.

"Like the one you're sporting, Fucko." Ricky chimed in, pointing at the guy's black eye.

The driver swerved dangerously close. Randall lunged, shoving Ricky off my bike. We tumbled over the curb together, bodies tangled but unharmed. Ricky's eyes flashed. He was up fast, grabbed a rock and chucked it sidearm style at their car. It smashed into the rearview window, dead center, leaving a spiderweb of cracks.

"Damn it," Ricky muttered as the car screeched to a halt. "Should have stayed in school!"

"Quick, get on!" I yelled.

We zigzagged through backyards and alleys, our hearts pounding in our chests. An unchained dog barked ferociously, trying to get through its fence as we sped past. We heard the car's tires screech; they were circling back.

"Go towards the hospital, then dip under the highway. They won't spot us on the tracks," Ricky suggested, his voice tinged with excitement.

As Ricky finished his sentence, I saw their car roar into the alley behind us. The engine revved, gravel flying as they floored it.

"They're gonna run us down!" Ricky screamed.

In a split-second decision, I veered hard left, cutting through a narrow path between two houses. The car skidded to a halt; doors slammed. Four guys, day drunk and wielding baseball bats, gave chase. But adrenaline fueled my legs. Ricky flipped them off as we sped away into the connecting street.

"Sit on that and rotate!" he yelled back.

We hit the downhill stretch, gaining speed and putting distance between us and them. Finally, I turned, and we ducked under the highway trestle, a makeshift sanctuary off the road. Gasping for air, we listened intently for any sign of their car.

"You think Troy gave that guy the black eye?"

"Has to be," I said, still catching my breath. "I don't know what his problem with Troy is."

"I knew his face looked familiar. I saw him visit Amanda before. He's a customer, probably fell in love, the poor bastard," said Ricky.

"How often do you go there, anyway?" I elbowed him.

Ricky's cheeks turned red. He was busted. I never saw that expression on his face before.

"Once in a while if I'm walking by or something."

I smiled at him, knowing full well he was lying.

"What?" he said, and then changed the subject. "They should know better than to come looking for trouble down here. If those asses are looking for a fight they came to the right town."

As we waited quietly under the trestle, I recalled how brutal fist fights were as normal as the change of seasons around here. I remember the first one I ever saw was right under that trestle. I was in 4th grade and the entire middle school knew a fight was agreed to and a location picked. It must have looked like we were heading to a class field trip because everyone walked in one big crowed divided into factions, chanting and hooting about who would kick who's ass that day. When everyone was under the trestle, we made a giant circle without anyone telling us to. Chants of "spread out, spread out!" as we made room for the two kids who had a score to settle. It was thrilling. They were 8th graders but to me they were grown men.

At first they circled one another, taunting and calling out for the other one to strike first. This dance didn't last long as the adrenaline was pumping through everyone's veins and you could feel it — the pressure for someone to come out a winner.

One kid, Eric something, was bigger but the kid who he was fighting was small, wiry, and was on the wrestling team. He dove down and took out Eric's legs with one move, doing a fireman's carry that put Eric on his back. From there fists started flying. You could hear their closed hands smacking each other hard in the face, the sides, it was crazy. Then there was blood, the smaller kid landed a solid hit on Eric's nose, and he went down begging for mercy. That's where I learned two important things about fights — it's always better to avoid a fight if you can, but if you can't, a straight punch with follow through that lands hard and direct is usually all it takes to settle. And that's why I hit Chad the way I did. The kids who lose fights all swing wild and throw punches like a windmill — the precision puncher won every fight I ever watched. Growing up in Snydersville you witness a lot them, especially if you are Troy McCloskey's kid brother. Troy kicked everyone's at ass at least once, but he gives the worst treatment to himself.

We only hung out until we were sure the coast was clear. Following under the trestle all the way to where it met the tracks, from there we split off and I kept my eyes peeled the whole way home.

I slammed the front door behind me. Troy was on the couch, beer in hand, engrossed in a stack of papers. He glanced up, his eyes narrowing as they took in my disheveled appearance.

"What the hell happened to you?" he asked, setting the papers aside as if they were suddenly less important.

"Man, you won't believe it. Some goons started tailing Ricky and me through town. They were asking about you," I said.

Troy's eyes darkened, like storm clouds rolling in. "Randall Jenkins and his merry band of idiots?"

"You know them?"

"Had to lay his ass out in front of Lucky's the other night. Guy's got a mouth that writes checks his fists can't cash."

"Well, they're here today, I mean he brought friends, and they're sniffing around for you and came after me and Ricky."

Troy clenched his fists, his knuckles turning white.

"If they so much as breathe on you, they'll regret it. I promise you that."

His protectiveness caught me off guard, but I knew he needed an excuse to fight someone and I was it, this time.

"Why the change of heart? Now you care what happens to me?"

Troy sighed, a heavy, burdened sound. He picked up the papers he'd been engrossed in earlier. "These are job applications, Pete. For the railroad factory. Apparently there's some work coming back, some French railroad company's gonna run the place. So I need your help little bro. I don't want to keep living like this forever, man."

"You need my help? With job applications?"

"Yeah. You've got a way with words, and I... well, I need this, Pete. It's my shot at something better, more, ya know, stable than....this." He spread his arms out, indicating the house we lived in.

For the first time, I looked at Troy not as my self-sabotaging alcoholic older brother, but as a man wrestling with his past, yearning for redemption and a new start like everyone else. The weight of years of bad choices hung heavy on his shoulders.

"Alright, I'll help you," I said, my voice softer, tinged with newfound respect.

Troy looked up, his eyes meeting mine. In that brief moment, the years of misunderstandings, the emotional distance that had grown between us, dissolved.

"Thanks, Pete. You have no idea how much this means to me."

We sat down, the job applications spread out on the coffee table before us like a roadmap to a better future. As I helped Troy navigate the labyrinth of questions and requirements, it felt as though we were also navigating the complexities of our fractured relationship. It felt like we were truly brothers again, bound not only by blood, but by a shared hope for a better tomorrow and a desire to help each other reach it.

TO BE A MAN

Climbing Big Creek Hill that afternoon was easier than ever before because my mind was so full of things I wanted to share that I barely remembered pedaling. When I chained my bike up to the entrance of Mapleton State Correctional Facility, I felt a lot better about myself than a few weeks ago. I didn't like hurting Chad, but I liked how he looked so weak and afraid after all those years of nonstop jokes, name calling and being a nonstop jerk to me. I couldn't wait to brag to my dad about that.

When he sat down, I leaned in closer to the divider, his eyes meeting mine. "You know, Dad, for the first time, I feel like I'm steering my own ship out here. I'm not reacting to life; I'm actually living it, like you said."

His eyes soften, a blend of pride, a bit of jealousy and deep regret. "That's what I've always wanted for you, Pete. To live life on your terms, not just survive it. That's all any parent should want for their kids."

"I stood up to that bully who's been making my life hell. I got suspended for it, but you know what? I don't care. I feel... liberated."

He looked at me with a mixture of concern and admiration. "Suspended, huh? This close to the end of school? Well, sometimes you've got to take a stand. Don't make a habit of it. You've got too much going for you, don't want to get a reputation like your old man."

"I can't escape your reputation, Dad. But it felt good to not be pushed around for once."

He leaned back, searching my eyes in a way I never experienced before, like he was looking to see if his temper was in me too.

"You're growing up, son. And I'm proud of you. Just promise me you'll always remember, every action has a reaction and a consequence. Make sure you can live with yours."

"I will. And I got some good news about Troy too. He picked up an application for some railroad work that's coming back, I'm working on it with him."

The hope in his eyes for Troy was clear. He loved his first born son who was the most like him. It hurt him that he never came up for a visit. He knew that Troy had become a bar room creature who lost hope.

"The railroad's hiring again, huh? That's solid work if he gets the job. It'll give him a future, something to build on."

"He's got a shot. I hope and pray that he gets hired. He needs this so bad."

"What about your future?"

"I take it one day at a time, but I think I might have some girlfriend potential starting now."

"You actually found someone who meets your high standards? I'm impressed," He remarked with a smile.

"It's that girl I told you about, Morgan, the one who helped me when I fell from my bike the other day. We're going on a date tonight. An actual, real, go meet somewhere date. I like Morgan a lot. She's different, you know? Smart, kind, and she listens and is always helping me for no reason. She's smarter than most of my teachers."

Dad leans in, a knowing smile on his face. "Ah, young love. Well, let me give you some advice, son. Always keep 'em guessing. Don't be too available."

I frown, not liking where this is going. "What do you mean?"

He chuckles. "You know, play a little hard to get. Women like the chase. They really do."

I shake my head, disagreeing. "That's not how I see it, Dad. Morgan's not some game to win. She's a person, and I respect her."

He looked puzzled, as if the concept was foreign to him.

"Respect is good, but don't you want to be the man in the relationship?"

"Being 'the man' doesn't mean I have to play games with her, does it?"

"That's the dating game, son. The dance is hard wired right into each of us."

"Sure, but I can still be honest, respectful, and treat her as an equal," I said.

He pondered this, scratching his stubbled chin. "Times have quickly changed out there, huh?"

I nod emphatically. "Morgan's going to college in New York City, aiming for big things. She inspires me."

Dad's eyes meet mine, and for a moment, I see a glimmer of him understanding where I'm coming from. He doesn't know Morgan but if he did I am sure he'd respect her too.

"Well, if she's as special as you say, don't let her slip away. But remember, relationships are a two-way street. Make sure she respects you too."

I lean in closer to the divider, wanting to make

sure he hears this next part clearly. "You know, Morgan's the first person who's ever treated me like I'm worth something. She doesn't look at me and see a screw-up or a McCloskey. She sees me, Pete."

Dad's eyes soften, and I can tell he's absorbing the weight of my words, knowing that he saddled me with the bad last name and reputation.

"That's rare, son. Hold onto that. Good people who see you for who you are don't come around often."

I nod, feeling a lump in my throat. "I know, Dad. I know."

We sit in silence for a moment, each lost in our own thoughts. I glanced at the clock on the wall and realize our time is almost up.

"Looks like they're about to call time," dad says, also noticing the clock.

"Yeah," I reply, feeling a sense of regret that our conversation has to end, but I did come later in the day than usual.

"Remember what we talked about, Pete. And give this Morgan girl a chance, but also give yourself a chance to be happy."

"I will, Dad. I promise."

The guard announces that visitation time is over, and we share a final look, a mix of understanding and hope passing between us, but the hope stayed with me and left him when the guard led him out of the room.

"See you, Dad," I say, my voice tinged with emotion.

"Take care, Pete. And keep living," he replied, echoing the advice he's given me before.

As I walked out of the visitation room, I felt a strange mixture of emotions. Excited about my future, especially the part that includes Morgan, but I'm also sad, thinking about the generational gaps and life lessons that only reveal themselves in moments of sadness and stress. I stepped out into the daylight, a sense of purpose filling me. I'm ready to live more, like dad said, but on my own terms from now on.

I mounted my bike, heading back into the life that's waiting for me, I realized that I'm suddenly looking forward to what comes next. On my way back over the hill to Snydersville, taking deep breaths and looking at the vast expanse of the clear sky above town, something weighed on my mind that I needed to face on my own.

I rode my bike through the quiet streets of the town, embracing the freedom it brought me. With each pedal, a sense of determination guided me, a belief in better things to come. I rounded a familiar corner, my destination came into view - Amanda's house, a source of intrigue and curiosity from the moment I knew what was going on.

Standing on Amanda's front porch in the middle of a sunny day, I felt a mix of anticipation, nervousness and embarrassment. Quietly, I knocked on the door, the sound echoing through the stillness of the day. I waited, my palms getting sweaty.

A curtain was pulled back. Amanda Breyer's eyes met mine before she cautiously opened the door, dressed in sweatpants and a faded Journey T-shirt.

"Pete McCloskey? What do you want?" she asked, her voice laced with curiosity and a hint of caution, her eyes looking past me to see if I was alone.

I collected myself, mustering my courage.

"I need to talk to you about Troy," I said, my voice steady but tinged with urgency.

Amanda sighed, leaning in the doorway. "Did he drink himself to death yet?"

I looked past her and noticed boxes half-packed

on the floor, their contents a jumble of memories and future plans. "No, he's at home. Are you moving?" I asked, momentarily distracted.

"Soon," she replied, avoiding eye contact.

"Troy's not gonna bother you anymore. I need to talk to you about him."

"Come in for a sec and sit down. You can talk to me while I pack."

I took a seat on her worn-out couch, its cushions bearing the imprints of countless evenings of adults having sex. Amanda sat across from me, her eyes searching mine as if trying to gauge my intentions. She lit a cigarette and took a puff, waiting for me to speak.

"Look, Amanda, I know you and Troy have had your issues, but he's really struggling and he's trying to get better. He hasn't been himself all year, and I think you're a big part of why."

She scoffed, rolling her eyes. "Each man makes his own problems, Pete. Troy's no different."

"But he still loves you, Amanda. You're the last thing in this world that I think he does love to be honest, more than even himself. Can't you see how much it's killing him that you won't give him another chance?"

Amanda looked at me, her eyes narrowing. "Love? You think this is about love? Troy's another drunk lost boy with a nice face in this town, like all the other once-good guys. He chooses his fate. He had his chances, plural."

I felt so frustrated knowing she was as petty as he was. "So what, you're going to let those goons keep him away from you? You think that's going to solve anything?"

She leaned back, crossing her arms. "Those 'goons,' as you call them, are doing that on their own. I never asked for their help."

I stared at her, disbelief washing over me. "You're really not going to do anything, are you?"

Amanda sighed, her eyes meeting mine. "Pete, I've got my own life to live now. I can't be responsible for Troy's happiness or his mistakes and neither can you."

I glanced at the half-packed boxes again, their presence suddenly making sense. "You're leaving Snydersville for good, aren't you? Running away from everything?"

She stood up, her eyes devoid of emotion. "I'm not running away, Pete. I'm moving on. There's a big difference."

I felt a knot tighten in my stomach. "And what about Troy? What's he supposed to do when the one thing he loves is gone for good?"

Amanda walked over to the window, staring out at the quiet middle school playground. "Troy's a grown man. He'll figure it out, or he won't. Either way, it's not my problem anymore."

I stood up, feeling defeated. "Alright, Amanda. If that's how you feel, then there's nothing more to say. I thought I'd try and prevent more sadness if possible."

As I walked towards the door, Amanda turned to me, her voice softer. "Pete, nobody is stuck here in the sadness. I hope you find what you're looking for in life, even if Troy never does."

"You too, Amanda. You too."

I stepped out into the sunlight, my bike waiting for me like an old friend. As I rode away, I knew that Snydersville was now a town with some people moving on, leaving behind those who couldn't—or wouldn't—

change. And as I pedaled through the streets, I made a silent promise to myself: I wouldn't be one of them. I will change and grow as much as I can.

When I returned home, Troy was gone for the night. I laid on my bed thinking about what Amanda said, about finding what I was looking for in life too, and how I could choose my own path. Right now the only path I wanted to be on was one that brought me closer to Morgan.

I splashed water on my face, styled my hair with some gel, brushed my teeth real good and made sure my pits didn't reek. I was trying hard to look and smell good for her. She only wanted to help me with school-work but I hoped she'd notice that I wasn't a total scumbag, just poor and unlucky to be stuck with my alcoholic brother.

I rode into downtown as the setting sun made the sky that orange color that makes the whole town glow. It was a magic hour that only happened on perfect days and this was one of them. All of my senses and all of my perceptions sharpened when I got cut loose from school. I didn't know what to make of it but I was feeling more connected and in control of the direction of every facet of my life. I passed the Pizza King where a couple of jocks were hanging around as always. I crossed the street to avoid them since that's Chad's group and they don't like me.

"Keep riding you fucking loser!" One of them yelled from across the street.

I raised my right hand and gave them the bird knowing nobody was going to touch me now that I broke Chad's nose. They could all jump me, and that's not out of the question around here, but I knew it would end any hopes many of them have for playing football next year.

I pulled up to the Texas Cafe and Morgan was already sitting alone in a booth. She waved and I had the biggest smile on my face — I could see it in the reflection — and felt stupid but I couldn't stop it.

Walking in I tried to look cool now that I was rocking a style. I flipped my jean jacket collar up and took one last peek at my reflection before going to her booth.

"Hi, Morgan, were you waiting long?"

"Nope, I got here early and went over your assignments that I picked from your teachers. Did you get a haircut?"

"I got some gel. Does it look weird like this?"

"No. It looks cool, like you're in a band."

I sat down feeling self-conscious in a good way. Did she like me—like me, or only like me as a friend, I could not tell.

Each booth had a little tabletop juke box on it, so I fished a nickel out of my pocket and started looking for a song to play.

"Pete we should get the work done before playing songs."

I kept flipping the song selection wheel on the side of the juke.

"I know. I was just checking what they got."

"It's all old music from the 50's. There's not one song in there that's modern," she said.

"What kind of music do you like?" I asked.

"All kinds, depends on the song."

"They have happy birthday," I said, as the waiter came over. He was the nephew of the owner and looked to be about sixty, but he was really in his thirties. He wore a white apron that was stained with chili and sauces that splashed when fixing the hot dogs.

"What do you kids want?" he said under his

breath, the odor of cigarettes and fry oil so strong
coming from him that I could taste it.

"Can I get one Texas hot and a small order of
fries?" said Morgan. Then he looked at me with his
eyebrows up and his frown down.

"My turn? I'll have the same, please."

"Drinks?" he snorted.

"Bottle of Coke for me," said Morgan.

"Same," I said again, feeling stupid that I didn't
have any originality whatsoever. She could have asked
for a mud pie with pebbles in a glass and I would have
ordered the same. Morgan smiled and opened a
trapper keeper she had on the seat beside her. "Let's
go over the assignments you need to complete and get
a passing grade on so you can get your diploma. It's
not as much work as it looks."

The wait for hot dogs felt like an eternity, each
second stretching out as if time itself was testing my
patience. Schoolwork had always been a struggle for
me, like a mental maze I couldn't navigate. My brain
short-circuited whenever I faced a sheet of questions
and problems. But then there was Morgan, this
beacon of clear thinking and sensitivity, guiding me
through the labyrinth of remedial math—the subject I
loathed the most but needed to pass desperately. Her
approach was gentle, devoid of any judgment, making
me feel like I was more than the sum of my academic
failures. She saw something in me, something I hadn't
even seen in myself. After we got through the work, I
had to ask.

"Why do you help me like this?" I was genuinely
puzzled, remembering that I am not even on her level.

"I don't want you to fail, and I know the system
isn't always fair to you," she replied, her eyes locking
onto mine.

Her words hit me like a freight train. She got it. She understood the skewed dynamics of our town and school, the invisible hurdles some of us had to jump to try and keep up.

"But why me? There are plenty of kids who probably won't graduate," I pressed.

"Because you have the smarts to make something of yourself. You're not like everyone else around here. You need a little push," she said.

I can't say I loved Morgan, but damn it, I loved Morgan. Right then and there, it was as if the universe had aligned itself for me to hear those encouraging words. No one had ever cared this much, had ever taken the time to believe in me like this. First, she'd patched up my physical wounds, and now she was healing parts of me I didn't even know were broken. I wanted to reciprocate, to be there for her, but what could she possibly need from someone like me?

"I don't even know how to thank you," I stammered.

"Always keep pushing forward and don't settle for mediocrity that defines so many. Aim higher, because life's short so we shouldn't waste it on living in the past," she advised, as our hot dogs arrived.

We pushed aside the worksheets, focusing on our meal. I fiddled with the jukebox, hitting play on a random selection. "Earth Angel" began to play, and I had to look away, afraid she'd see right through me. The lyrics resonated with what I was feeling.

Earth angel, Earth angel, will you be mine?
My darling dear, love you all the time.
I'm just a fool, a fool in love with you.

The song was a relic from a simpler era, a time I

found myself yearning for more and more. Morgan embodied that simplicity, that purity. As our makeshift homework date came to an end, it dawned on me why she'd remained single, why she didn't mingle much with people our age. She was an old soul, like me. I'd always felt out of place, like a man born in the wrong time, but being with her made me feel seen, understood. We had a connection.

It was a strange and exhilarating sensation, one that filled me with hope and fear. Could I make myself into the man she deserved? Could I elevate myself to be worthy of her?

"I have not had a Texas hot in a long time. I forgot how good these are," Morgan said, her eyes wide with delight.

"Me too. I don't usually eat dinner," I said. We had been there all of an hour but it felt so much longer in a good way. In fact I never wanted to leave the warmth of the cafe, the chatter of other customers and their songs playing softly from the table jukes and me sitting with Morgan doing homework.

"Chad always had it out for you, hasn't he?" Morgan asked, her eyes narrowing as if she were trying to solve a puzzle.

"Yeah, ever since fourth grade. But the moment he found out my dad was in jail, he's been relentless. It's like he's got a vendetta against me for something that's not even my fault," I explained, feeling the weight of years of pent-up frustration coming out.

"I remember that," Morgan said, her eyes drifting to a distant memory. "You know, back in grade school, Chad cornered you during recess one day. He was about to really lay into you."

I nodded, recalling the incident. "Yeah, I remember. Mrs. Thompson came out of nowhere and broke it up. Saved my skin that day."

Morgan smiled, a little mysteriously. "Actually, I was the one who ran to get Mrs. Thompson. I couldn't stand there and watch you get bullied. You did nothing to instigate it."

I looked at her, stunned. "You did that? Wow, you've been looking out for me longer than I realized."

She shrugged modestly. "Someone had to. You're not the only one with family issues either. My uncle's in the county jail right now for bouncing checks. Chronic offender. It's like a disease that runs in the family or something."

"Seems like everyone around here is struggling in some way. Doesn't it feel like we're stuck on a sinking ship?" I said.

"That's exactly why I have to leave for New York City for school," Morgan said, her tone tinged with a sadness I hadn't detected before. "I can't stay here and let this place drag me down. I must make a life elsewhere, somewhere I can actually have a future doing what I want."

I nodded, understanding her urgency. "It's like we're all in quicksand, and you've found a branch to pull yourself out. I'm glad you're taking it, Morgan. Don't let this place hold you back."

She looked at me, her eyes softening. "Pete. You deserve better than this too."

I felt a lump in my throat. "Maybe one day I...but for now, I've got to figure out how to settle into my own life here."

Morgan smiled, and for a moment, I felt like everything was going to be okay. Even if she was leaving, even if I was stuck here, we had this moment, a moment where two old souls discovered a kinship and found solace in a world that often was too harsh to bear. As we wrapped up our dinner, I started fantasizing about a future where she and I were more than friends. Maybe if I worked hard enough, if I continued to evolve, she'd want to be a part of my life in a way that transcended friendship when she came home from college.

We left the Texas Cafe, the air outside tinged with the sweet scent of fried onions and chili from the roof vent. I began to unchain my bike, but noticed Morgan wasn't heading to her car.

"Where'd you park?"

"My mom went to play bingo, so I walked over," she replied, her voice soft like the evening breeze.

"In that case, would you like a lift?" I offered, gesturing to the pegs on my bike's back wheels. "I can steer one-handed, you know. Let me carry the trapper keeper."

Her eyes lit up, and she handed me the trapper keeper. As she moved behind my bike and her hands gently grasped my shoulders, I felt empowered. It was as if her calming touch had imbued me with an invincible new sense of self-assurance. I looked back at her, our eyes locking for a moment.

"Ready?" I asked.

"Ready," she confirmed.

With a gentle push, we were off, Morgan balancing gracefully on the pegs. Gliding through the downtown streets with her felt like a dream, as if we had crossed some unspoken boundary. The thought of love filled me with a sense of hope and wonder.

As we crossed Main Street, the warm, yellow glow of the streetlights bathed us in a golden aura, lighting up the canopy of maple trees that lined the side streets. Their leaves rustled softly in the night wind, as if whispering secrets to each other as we passed. The town was quiet over here, leaving us alone in this dreamlike state.

But as we cut down Maple Street, heading towards her house, reality intruded. I spotted that same car that had chased Ricky and me earlier in a driveway. There was a party going on inside with people on the porch. As we passed, the guys who had been looking for Troy spotted me, their eyes locking onto mine.

"Hey, that's McCloskey right there," one of them called out, shattering the magical spell of the evening.

"Hang on, Morgan. These guys are after me."

They ran to their car as we shot down the street. Morgan held on to my chest tightly.

"Who are they?"

"Some jerks that have a problem with Troy and now they're after me too."

Within seconds their headlights of grew larger in my peripheral vision. My heart was pounding, not from the exertion alone, but from the fear of what these guys might do, especially with Morgan with me. I couldn't let anything happen to her; she meant too much to me.

"Turn here!" Morgan shouted, pointing to a narrow side street that connected to the back lot behind an abandoned furniture store. I swerved hard, my tires skidding on the asphalt. The car roared past, momentarily confused before slamming on the breaks and reversing at full speed.

We reached the lot and I steered the bike behind a dumpster. Morgan and I got off, crouched down and waited, our breath shallow and quick, listening as the car circled back and drove right into the back lot, its engine growling like an animal on the hunt. The engine grew louder until it was a few feet from the dumpster, headlights flickering through the gaps in the dumpster, casting eerie shadows on the cracked walls of the old building. Morgan's eyes met mine, wide with fear but also a glimmer of excitement and defiance. I put a finger to my lips, signaling for her to stay quiet. We could see them through the small gap where the lid didn't close all the way.

The car's engine idled for what felt like an eternity. Finally, the door creaked open and heavy boots hit the ground. "Where'd they go?" one of the goons grumbled, his voice tinged with frustration.

"I don't know, man, but when I find that kid, I'm gonna—" The other goon's words were cut off as his eyes landed on my bike, the front wheel still partially visible and sticking out the other side of the dumpster. A cruel smile spread across his face. "Well, well, what do we have here?"

He stomped over to my bike and yanked it out from its hiding spot. "Looking for this?" he sneered, holding it up like a trophy. They found us, so we walked out form behind the dumpster.

That bike was more than a means of transportation; it was my freedom, my escape from the chaos of life in Snydersville. I couldn't let them take it away from me. I lunged at the goon grabbing my bike in a tug of war. We both pulled on one wheel.

"Give that to me!"

Caught off guard, he stumbled back, and we both dropped the bike with a clatter. I heard the engine revving and I sprang into action, grabbing Morgan and shielding her body. The car accelerated and ran right over my bike. The frame crunched under the tires, spokes flew in all directions.

I saw a figure on the bridge to the right of us. It was Troy, my brother, unmistakable even in the dim light. He was looking down, and I knew he'd seen the whole thing. Without a second thought, he started sprinting down the bridge's slope, right onto the riverbank that connected to the lot, his face set in a grim line.

Troy reached the parking lot as the goons climbed back into their car looking for something. He didn't hesitate. With a roar, he pounced on the first guy, landing a solid kick on the door that crushed his leg. The second guy got out and swung a bat, but Troy dodged and countered with a vicious uppercut that laid his ass out. Then he took his bat.

"Get out of here, Pete! Take her and go!" Troy yelled, his eyes meeting mine for a split second.

I didn't need to be told twice. Grabbing the trapper keeper and Morgan's hand, we ran out of the parking lot and down the side street at full speed, my brother's shouts and the sounds of a bad scuffle fading behind us. The insults and taunts echoed in the night. Then I heard a distant siren and knew the police were on the way.

Out on the street, I looked back one last time to see Troy standing there clubbing the biggest guy in the leg, over and over again while he begged for mercy. The two other guys were on the ground, clutching their bodies, reeling in pain. He looked up and our eyes met. In that moment, I felt a mix of fear, gratitude, and a newfound respect for my brother who could and did kick anyone's ass who tried him. He'd always been a tough guy, but tonight he was my hero.

Morgan grabbed my shoulder, shaken by all of it. "We should keep walking, get away from here."

"Yeah, you don't need this. I'm sorry, Morgan."

As we walked, I couldn't help but think about how close we'd come to real danger, and how much I owed Troy. And how screwed I was going to be with no bike.

"We're almost there, are you going to be ok?" Morgan said, breaking the silence that had settled between us. Her voice was soft, but it carried a weight, a shared understanding of the night's events.

"I'll be fine. Thanks for...you know, sticking by me back there."

She smiled, "You protected me, Pete. I should be thanking you."

I looked down, my eyes tracing the cracks in the sidewalk. "I'm really screwed without my bike, you know? It was more than a way to get around. It was my ticket to freedom, my escape from all the crap at home."

"You need a ride somewhere tomorrow?"

I hesitated, uncomfortable with the idea of revealing too much. "Well, I do need to go to this place, and it's kind of an emergency now, but it's not exactly close."

She tilted her head, curious but not pressing. "If you need a lift, I can help out. I have the car tomorrow and I liked being with you tonight."

I looked at her, torn. I didn't want her to get more involved in the mess that was my life, but I also knew I needed to get where I needed to go. Finally, I decided to come clean. "Look. I need to talk to my dad about what to do with Troy because if the cops came, that boy is in jail now and he ain't getting out."

"Your dad's up in Mapleton?"

"Yeah, Mapleton."

Morgan's eyes softened, "I'll drive you there first

thing in the morning and then we can do more schoolwork. How's that sound?"

I felt a warmth spread through me, a sense of gratitude and relief that was new but welcome. "Alright, you've got a deal. Thank you, Morgan."

At Morgan's house, the atmosphere changed. The night, which had been so full of life and promise, suddenly felt heavy with the weight of an impending journey to a bad place in the morning.

I handed her the trapper keeper since she was going to turn in my work. She hugged it between both arms, looking at me as if I was missing a beat.

"So, um, I guess I'll see you in the morning?" I finally managed to stammer out, my eyes darting to meet hers.

"Yeah, I'll see you then," she smiled back to me.

I was relieved but still struggling with the awkwardness of the moment. "I really appreciate all your help, Morgan. You're making a big difference for me. You have no idea..."

She smiled, I stopped talking, and for a moment, the weight of goodbye lifted.

"I'm glad I can help, Pete. You're worth it and I like you."

"I like you too. I like you a lot," I said, unable to find more words. That's when she kissed me on the forehead, short and sweet, then turned to walk up the steps to her front door. I felt a longing I couldn't quite define. I watched as she reached her door, turned the knob, and paused. She looked back at me, her eyes meeting mine one last time.

"Goodnight, Pete," she said, her voice carrying a soft promise of many more nights to come.

"Goodnight, Morgan," I replied, my voice barely above a whisper.

She stepped inside and closed the door behind her, I turned around and ran back to check on Troy, my thoughts a haze of emotions. But through it all, one thing was clear: tomorrow my dad was going to meet my girlfriend.

As I rounded the corner back to the lot, out of breath and sweating hard, my fears were confirmed: the flashing red and blue lights of police cars and an ambulance painted the scene in a surreal, nightmarish glow. Something very bad went down.

I leaned against a maple tree, my eyes in disbelief at the sight before me. The ambulance doors were closing, and I couldn't see who was inside. My heart sank. Was it one of the guys Troy had fought? Was it Troy himself? I couldn't tell, and the uncertainty gnawed at me. Paramedics were working on whoever it was, so at least I knew they were alive.

Then I saw him in the back of a squad car, his face a mixture of anger and resignation. From my vantage point across the street, hidden in the shadows, I watched as Troy's frustration boiled over. He banged his head against the seat divider in front of him, not once, but multiple times. Each thud was like a punch to my gut, a reminder of the life we were both trying to escape but somehow couldn't.

The police officers got into the car, and as they drove away, Troy looked out the window but didn't see me. I felt a profound sense of loss. My brother was being taken away, swallowed up by a system that had been against us from the start. And as a repeat offender with the last name McCloskey, I knew the odds were stacked against him.

I stood there, alone, long after the flashing lights had disappeared, grappling with a new harsh reality. Despite our best efforts, despite our dreams of something better, we were still products of our environment, still caught in a cycle we couldn't seem to break.

As I turned to leave for the long walk home, my thoughts returned to Morgan, to the idea of a better future that she represented. It felt more distant than ever, a faint glimmer, swallowed up by the darkness of the night. I couldn't wait for morning to arrive.

THE LONELIEST ROAD

The engine of Morgan's car hummed softly as we drove through the empty streets of Snydersville in the early morning, right as daylight was beginning to break, casting a soft pink glow over the town. It should've been a peaceful morning, but my insides were a tangled knot of nerves. I didn't sleep at all, feeling awful that Morgan was getting roped into my drama, but I had no choice but to take her up on the offer. I caught myself biting my nails, a nervous habit I couldn't seem to shake.

Morgan glanced over at me, her eyes filled with understanding. "You okay, Pete?"

"Yeah," I lied, forcing a smile. "There's a lot on my mind, you know, worried about Troy and all."

She nodded, her gaze returning to the road as we turned right and began the climb up Big Creek Hill. "It's not every day you have to visit someone in a place like Mapleton."

My eyes drifted to the window, to the passing fields and farms. "I've been there a lot. My dad's always been the one I turn to for advice. Especially when it comes to dealing with Troy's messes. And now, with Troy arrested and God knows what else happening, he's the only one I can talk to."

Morgan's hand found mine, giving it a reassuring squeeze. "Hey, it's okay. You shouldn't be ashamed for something you didn't do. What happened a long time ago is not your fault."

I looked at her, really looked at her, and felt a sense of gratitude wash over me. "That means a lot."

As we reached the summit of Big Creek Hill, I felt the car shift gears, preparing for the descent into the valley where Mapleton State Correctional Facility loomed like a fortress. I took a deep breath, bracing myself for the emotional toll the visit would undoubtedly take. The prison's imposing structure became a dark monument against the morning sky.

My heart pounded in sync with the engine as we pulled to the gate, where the car came to a halt beside the guardhouse. The guard, a middle-aged man with a gruff exterior but kind eyes, recognized me immediately. "Morning, Pete. Who's this?" he asked, nodding toward Morgan.

"This is Morgan. She gave me a ride today, my bike got run over." I replied, my voice tinged with nervousness.

The guard looked us both over, then picked up his radio. "Control, this is the front gate. The McCloskey kid is here, and he's got company."

A crackling voice responded, "Roger that, hold them there for a moment."

We sat in an uneasy silence, the tension palpable. Morgan squeezed my hand again, as if to say, "I'm here for you, no matter what."

A different guard emerged from the main building, walking briskly toward us. He was younger, with a stern face that looked like it rarely smiled. "Mr. Mc-

Closkey, if you and your friend could park in one of these spots and then follow me," he said, his tone formal, almost rehearsed.

I looked at Morgan, my eyes filled with questions. It's never been this way before at the gate. She gave me a nod, parked nearby and we both got out of the car.

The guard led us into the prison through a series of heavy doors and long hallways, each one more sterile and unwelcoming than the last. Finally, he ushered us into a small room, separate from the usual visiting area. It was stark, with a desk and three chairs. The atmosphere felt heavy, like the room was holding its breath.

"Please have a seat," the guard said, gesturing to the chairs. "Someone will be with you shortly to discuss some matters."

Morgan and I sat down, our eyes meeting for a moment before we both looked away. The weight of the situation was sinking in, and I felt a knot tighten in my shoulders.

The door opened again. This time the warden appeared from around a corner and as he approached, my senses heightened. Each step he took amplified the dread that had settled in my bones. I knew, even before he spoke, that something had irrevocably changed. The air was thick with it.

The warden sat on the desk. His eyes met mine, and I felt a chill run down my spine.

"Pete, I'm afraid I have some bad news," he began, his voice tinged with a gravity that made my stomach drop. "Your father... he's gone. He took his own life last night." His face was stern, but his eyes betrayed a certain sadness.

"What do you mean?" I pleaded, tears coming down my face. Morgan held my hand, but I pulled away and covered my face. "What do you mean? Why?"

"Prison is a dead end, son. I'm sorry he left you alone like this."

His words hurt like hell, cutting my heart up like a razor. I wanted to vomit. I wanted to die. I didn't want to be there with Morgan. She moved close and hugged me, rocking me like the broken child I was. "It's okay. It's okay."

I bawled until there was nothing left.

The warden handed me a manila envelope with my dad's name on it, "William McCloskey." Inside were his final belongings—a gold watch, pictures of our family in happier times, personal letters, and papers. I clutched the envelope to my chest, feeling utterly lost. The warden offered me a tissue and a cup of water, muttering condolences and saying it was a sad reality of prison life.

Nothing felt real, yet everything felt realer than real. Morgan shared in my sadness, taking it on when she didn't have to. She rubbed my shoulders and kept whispering that it was ok and I would be ok.

My father, the man who had been my rock, my personal source of wisdom in a world that often made no sense, was suddenly gone. Like that. My body and mind felt detached, like I could see myself in the third person, sitting there, wondering what to do. I thought about Troy, about the path he was on, and how it looked frighteningly similar to the one my dad had walked. I couldn't save my dad, but maybe I could still save Troy.

As we pulled away from the prison, I felt like I was leaving behind a piece of my soul, trapped within those walls that had witnessed the shattering of my world. Morgan drove in silence, allowing me the space to grieve. When we reached the summit of Big Creek Hill, she pulled over into a small clearing. It was a secluded spot under a weeping willow, a few yards from the road.

"What are you doing?"

"Let's do nothing for as long as we need to," she said.

We sat there, looking down into the valley below where Snydersville lay. From up here, the town looked so small, so inconsequential, and yet it was my entire life—filled with joys and sorrows, love and loss, and pain. Especially pain.

"It's the pain that's hardest to forget," I finally said, breaking the silence.

Morgan turned her gaze to me. Her eyes were soft but steady, as if she were trying to share some of her own hard learned resilience.

"You're right, Pete. Pain is the common thread that weaves through all our lives. But it's not the only one. There's love, friendship, and moments of genuine happiness in simple things like sitting under a tree together."

I looked at her, appreciating her voice. "Yeah, but those moments seem so fleeting."

"Life is real good at handing out unwanted baggage, Pete. Heavy, cumbersome baggage filled with our past mistakes, our regrets, and our sorrows. And the world? It expects us to carry it, to be weighed down by it everywhere we go."

I felt a lump form in my throat. "So what are we supposed to do then? Keep lugging it around for all of eternity?"

"The key to happiness, to really living free, is learning how to set that baggage down. You don't have to carry it, not if you don't want to. That's the part nobody tells you. I had to figure that out by myself."

As we sat there, the weight of the moment settling over us, I realized that even in the darkest of times, there were glimmers of light found in other people. And sometimes, those glimmers were enough to guide you through the darkness.

I asked Morgan to drop me off at the Snydersville Police Department, and I told her I would take it from here and keep her posted. I didn't want her good name associated with my bad one. She gave me a big hug and kissed me on the cheek before I stepped out. "You got this," she said.

She pulled away. I steeled myself and walked in, my Converse squeaking on the just-mopped linoleum floor. The officer behind the desk looked up, his eyes narrowing as he recognized me.

"You're here for Troy McCloskey?"

"Yeah," I said, my voice tinged with urgency. "What's it gonna take to get him out?"

The officer flipped through some papers before landing on a sheet. "Bail's set at five grand this time."

Five thousand dollars. That was a fortune. I remembered my secret stash, the money I'd been saving for years for something important. This was it. This was the important thing. I nodded, trying to keep my composure. "Alright, I'll be back."

I raced home on foot and went right to the old oak tree in our backyard, its branches like outstretched arms. I used my finger to trace a line from the Troy and Amanda engraving all the way to the bottom of the trunk. Using a rock, I tapped gently around the bark until a chunk popped out. I dug behind it, my fingers scraping against the familiar tin box. My life savings, all kept for a moment like this. I opened it, the

wad of cash staring back at me. It was about everything I had to my name, but what good was money if I
couldn't help my own brother? I pocketed the cash,
got back on my road and walked down to the jail.

"I've got the money," I said, laying the wad of cash
on the counter.

The officer counted it, his eyes widening slightly as
he realized I had the full amount. "Alright, we'll start
the process to get him released. Have a seat."

As I waited in the sterile, dimly lit area of the city
jail, my eyes fixed on the heavy door that separated
the inmates from the outside world, a gnawing fear
came over me. I couldn't save my dad, but I had a
chance to set Troy straight. Yet, the thought that he
might never change bothered me. Troy was high risk,
a wild card. He was as likely to hug me when he walks
through that door, as he was to throw a punch as if
we're in a bar fight. But he was my brother, and the
emotional tether that bound us was still intact on my
end. I needed to hug him, to feel a family connection
that was tangible and not out of reach. We had been
so fractured and strained over the years. I needed to
know that despite the chaos, the McCloskey blood ran
true in both of us.

My throat thickened and my chest tightened as I
heard footsteps approaching. The heavy door creaked
open, and there he was—Troy, looking disheveled but
unmistakably relieved to be on this side of the bars.
Our eyes met, and in that moment, all the unspoken
words, all the pent-up emotions, hung in the air between us.

I stood up, my legs felt like they were made of lead.
I walked over to him, my eyes never leaving his. And
then, without a word, I hugged him. I hugged him
with all the strength and love and desperation that I

felt. It was a hug that said, "I'm here for you," but also, "I need you not to mess this up." As we stood there, locked in that embrace, I let it out.

"Dad's gone now too, Troy," I finally managed to say, my voice breaking. "He took his own life, hung himself. He wanted to be free."

Troy's face remained stoic, his eyes not betraying any emotion. But I felt him grip me a little tighter, as if holding onto a lifeline.

We emerged from the dimly lit jailhouse into the warming sun, its brightness almost too much for our eyes to bear. I walked alongside Troy in silence, our heads bowed as if weighed down by the drama of our lives.

Troy's boot connected with a stray rock, sending it skittering across the pavement. He muttered something under his breath, a low growl of frustration, and shook his head as if trying to dispel demons that haunted him.

As we approached the bridge that marked the boundary between us and the rest of the world, I stopped walking. Troy took a few more steps before realizing I wasn't beside him. He turned back, his face a canvas of exhaustion and resignation.

"You coming?" he asked, his voice tinged with a vulnerability he never showed.

"We can't keep living like this, Troy,"

"I was defending you, Pete. Those guys would've messed you up bad. Could have killed you."

"I know, and that's why I emptied my entire savings to bail you out. But now, you've got to fight for yourself, for us. We're all we've got, Troy. We're alone in this world." My voice cracked, and I felt the tears welling up, blurring my vision. "And I don't know how much more of this bullshit I can take."

Troy retraced his steps until he was standing beside me. We walked to the edge of the bridge and sat there, side by side, staring down at the river below. It was as if the water carried away years of unspoken pain, years of bottled-up emotions.

We opened up about the past that had hurt us both, about the longing for a mother's love and a father's guidance—things we never had but always yearned for. We talked about the void that had been growing inside us, a void we had tried to fill with anger and rebellion. It was a cathartic moment, a release of years of emotions, and despite the heaviness that hung over us, I felt a new connection with Troy. It was a feeling of companionship, of shared pain and shared hope, akin to what I felt around Morgan, yet distinct in its own right. I felt a little less alone in the world on a day that began with my world ending.

Later, Mr. Stilson pulled up to my house in his Buick, the engine idling as he stepped out and made his way to the front door with a large crockpot filled with pasta. When he heard about my dad, he insisted on coming over to check on me. "Take some time, Pete. The store will manage without you for a few days," he said, his eyes filled with a kind of understanding that only comes knowing someone well.

I took his advice to heart. Ricky and Little T. stopped by and kept me company, their presence a welcome distraction from the emptiness that had settled on me. Even Troy was changed by the gravity of our loss, finally taking the initiative to clean up the house and get rid of the junk that had accumulated over the years. That weekend Troy and I worked to rebuild my bike with new rims and handlebars. Little by little, things were getting put back together.

By the following Monday, I was back working at

Stilson's, the familiar scent of liquor and wood filling the air as I neatened up the shelves. The routine was comforting, a small island of normalcy in the storm.

The door chime rang, waking me from my thoughts. I looked up to see Morgan walking in, her eyes scanning the store before landing on me.

"Hey, Morgan, it's good to see you," I said, setting down a bottle of bourbon and walking over to her. We hugged and it felt good, warm. I'd been avoiding her all week, not because I didn't like her—by that point I knew I loved her—because I knew she was leaving, and I didn't want to feel another loss.

"How have you been, Pete? How's your brother? I've been looking for you."

"I'm getting through it, you know? One day at a time. I'm thankful you were there for me," I said. "How is it getting ready to move?"

She hesitated, her eyes meeting mine. "Well...I found out that I'm approved to move in early to get to know the city a little before classes begin. I'm so excited to think I'll be living in Greenwich Village soon."

"You've got a lot of amazing different times ahead."

"And what about you?" she inquired. "What's next now that things have settled down a bit?"

"Oh, I've got my work cut out for me right here. Troy and I are planning to rehab the house. It's not Greenwich Village, but it's something."

Morgan reached into her bag and pulled out an envelope. "I brought you this," she said, handing it over. "You skipped the ceremony, so I figured you might want your diploma."

"With my dad and all, I totally forgot about graduation. Thanks, Morgan."

I opened the envelope and looked at the diploma, its embossed letters and official signatures suddenly seeming so inconsequential after all that pressure and anxiety over getting it. "I don't know how much use this will be for me."

"It's not about its utility, Pete. It's a mile marker, not the defining achievement of your life. You crossed it. We crossed it. Together."

She always made good points and they always made me more attracted to her. "Maybe I'll visit NYC someday, see what all the fuss is about. I've never been away from here."

"You should," she encouraged. "NYC is a school all by itself. Being there gives me such energy it's amazing. Remember Pete, if you let go of the baggage, you can go anywhere too."

"I'm trying, especially now that you've shown me it's possible."

"That's all you can do, Pete. Just try."

Ricky looked up from stacking bottles and gave me a nod, a silent acknowledgment that spoke volumes. He agreed with her.

"I will," I assured her. "Try not to forget me," I joked.

"I won't," she said.

Morgan smiled, her eyes lingering on mine for a moment longer. "I have to go. My bus leaves early on Monday morning. But I'll be back for the holiday break, and I can't wait to see what you guys do to your house."

We shared one final hug and I didn't want to let go. As she walked out, the door chime ringing behind her, I felt the weight of the crossroads we were at. She was stepping into a new chapter, one filled with danger, opportunities and challenges I could only imagine. And me? I was here, in Snydersville, coming to terms with my own predictable set of challenges with no real opportunities.

Mr. Stilson came from his back office, caught my eye, then gestured for me to follow him outside.

We stepped into the parking lot, the sun casting long shadows as the day wore on. Mr. Stilson leaned against his Buick that had seen better days but still ran like a dream. He looked at me with a mix of compassion and understanding that only comes from years of knowing someone.

"Pete, I've been thinking a lot about your dad. I'm really sorry, son," he began, his voice tinged with regret. "Life has a way of burying us alive at times, doesn't it? I hope you understand it's not the first time something like that has happened up at Mapleton, and it won't be the last. That's why you've got to keep busy with good things, with living, keep moving forward. Don't let life bog you down no matter how hard it tries. That's what your dad would have wanted for you."

I nodded, taking in his words. Mr. Stilson reached into his car and pulled out a manila envelope, handing it to me with a solemn expression.

"I've been thinking a lot about what comes next, for me and for this place. You've been like a son to me all these years, Pete. You've got a good head on your shoulders, and you've got the grit to make something better than it was when you found it. So, I want you to have this."

I opened the envelope and pulled out a legal document. It took me a moment to process what I was seeing. It was the deed to the liquor store building, along with papers indicating the full ownership of the business would be mine.

"Mr. Stilson, I... I don't know what to say," I stammered, overwhelmed by the enormity of his gift.

"Don't say anything, Pete. Take it and make it your own. My wife and I decided its time we move to Florida. We've had our stay here, and now it's your turn to mind the shop."

I looked up at him. In that moment I felt a sense of responsibility, not only for the store but for my own life and now Ricky's too. Mr. Stilson had given me more than a business; he'd given me a ready-made future, a chance to build something meaningful with this big gift. And as I stood there, sunshine glaring off the car and catching my eyes, I knew that I would honor this gift, not for Mr. Stilson alone, but for myself, for Troy, and for everyone else who believed in me and gave me a chance.

When I got home, the sun was setting, casting a warm glow through the cracks in the curtains. Troy was in the kitchen, scrubbing dishes like he was trying to erase the past. He really did quit drinking cold turkey. I was impressed. It was not easy to witness but he was past the worst of it now and kept himself busy at all times while he awaited a reply from the railroad. I knew he was hoping to get hired and have the work take over his entire life, but sensed he was afraid that if it didn't come through he would be in worse shape than before, and I shared that fear. Troy needed a purpose too. We all do. When your family tree is busted at the root and no water makes it to the leaves, you can't grow because you don't know how. You never find your purpose.

RUST BELT BLUES

I n the days that followed, Ricky and I found ourselves in the familiar setting of the open space behind the Larson trailer, BB gun in hand, taking turns shooting at tin cans we'd set up on an old wooden fence. We hadn't done this since ninth grade and now we had some time since Mr. Stilson was still minding the store for one final week. The sun was high, casting long shadows that danced with each can we knocked off its perch.

"So, now that you officially own the store, does that mean I'm getting a raise?" Ricky asked, squinting down the barrel before letting a BB fly. The can tumbled off the fence.

"Could be," I said, pondering the future that was suddenly so full of possibilities. "Depends on how the summer goes, how the store does. I still have to learn how to run the business alone from Mr. Stilson."

Ricky chuckled, handing me the BB gun. "Well, one thing's for sure, I ain't calling you Mr. McCloskey, boss or not."

"Don't worry," I assured him, taking aim and firing. "You'd never have to do that with me."

As I reloaded, Ricky shifted the conversation. "So,

what's the deal with you and Morgan? I thought you two were turning into an item."

I handed the gun back to him. "I wish. She's off to New York for college on Monday. She'll be back after the first semester, but who knows if she'll remember me when she comes home? A lot can change. There's a lot of people in NYC."

Ricky took aim but paused, locking eyes with me. "You know, Pete, you better not let her get too far away. Girls like her don't come around often and help a guy like she did with you. From what I've seen, she's into you, man. Really into you, as crazy as that seems."

"It is crazy and I kinda still don't believe it," I added, then leaned against the fence, my eyes tracing the outlines of the tin cans, each one representing a choice, a path, a future. Ricky's words echoed in my mind, amplifying the internal debate I'd been having with myself about Morgan.

Handing the BB gun back to me, Ricky added, "Actions speak louder than words, Pete. She's been there for you, hasn't she? That's gotta mean something."

Ricky was right. Morgan had been there for me in ways no one else had and at the right time in my life. I pulled the trigger, and as the can clattered to the ground, I knew what I had to do. It was a long shot, maybe even a crazy one, but it was a shot I was willing to take.

As I biked home through the streets of Snydersville, the town unfolded before me like a well-worn book, each landmark a chapter in my simple small town life. I passed the bars where my brother Troy used to hang out, the school where I'd struggled and triumphed, the barber shop that doubled as a bus stop, and the Texas Cafe. Each place felt both intimately familiar and strangely distant, as if I was seeing them through new eyes.

The realization that these places, these memories, were all part of my past, and the past, if clung to too tightly, becomes a haunting ground for ghosts. Ghosts that could chain you, hold you back, keep you from living your own life going forward.

I had planned to stop by Morgan's house, but something inside me shifted. Instead, I went straight home with thoughts that needed to be put down on paper.

I sat at the kitchen table, took out a sheet of paper, and began to write. My hand moved almost of its own accord, pouring out words that had been locked inside me for too long. It was emotional, cathartic, and as I wrote, I felt as if I was releasing a part of myself that had been held captive until now.

Troy walked in, a smile on his face that I hadn't seen in years. His eyes were clear and his whole vibe was lighter "Guess what, Pete? I got hired by the new railroad company. Can you believe it?"

"That's amazing, Troy! I'm so proud of you, man. When do you start?"

"I start training on Monday. This Monday." He leaned over to see what I was working on. "What are you doing, turning into a writer now?"

His news added a new meaning to the letter I was writing but I didn't want him to read it so I covered it up. It was as if the universe was aligning, telling me that the time for change, for growth, for new beginnings, was now so don't miss it.

"It's for a special friend."

"Your girlfriend?" She's cute, Pete. Don't let her get away."

I smiled and folded the letter carefully, sealing it in

an envelope. Its contents known only to me. And as I looked at that envelope, peace washed over me. I was finally unburdened by the ghosts of my past.

Monday came and I imagined Troy up and getting ready for his first day at the railroad, probably too busy to look around for me. But I wasn't there. Instead, I was on my bike, an overstuffed backpack slung over my shoulders, pedaling like my life depended on it. My heart pounded in sync with the rhythm of the wheels, each pump taking me further away from my past and closer to an uncertain future that was calling me.

I reached the downtown bus stop in time to see Morgan standing there with her luggage, ready to board the bus to New York City when it arrives. Right behind her was Amanda, with a couple of different boxes affixed to a pull cart.

They didn't see me until my bike clattered when I leaned it against a street sign pole, my eyes locking onto Morgan's.

"Pete? What are you doing here?" she asked, her eyes widening in surprise.

"I'm coming with you," my voice confident and sure of myself like never before. "I mean, can I come with you? I gotta get out of here."

"To New York City?

"I can't stay here, Morgan. There's no future for me in a town that keeps me stuck living in the past. I'll work hard, find a job. I know I can make it."

Morgan looked at me, her eyes searching mine, and then she smiled—a smile that held understanding, acceptance, and perhaps a hint of shared dreams.

"Life's an adventure better had with a friend. You

can crash with me until school starts. Let's figure it out together, explore New York together," she said.

"Good for you two." said Amanda, smiling at us. "Get out of this town and go make something of your lives. I'm happy for you."

I turned to Amanda. "I'm happy for you too. You deserve better. We all deserve better," I said, elated and smiling from ear to ear.

Just then, the bus rounded the corner, its large frame pulling into the stop with a hiss of air brakes. The door swung open, and the driver stepped out onto the sidewalk.

"Snydersville," he announced, before collecting tickets and assisting with luggage.

Morgan handed over her ticket, and the driver began stowing her bags in the undercarriage of the bus. Amanda did the same, her boxes fitting snugly into the remaining space. I handed over my ticket, my backpack joining the pile, its weight suddenly lifted in more ways than one.

As the driver climbed back into his seat and the door hissed closed, I sat next to Morgan, our hands finding each other as the bus pulled away.

It only took a few turns through town and then one long road out. Stilson's was the last thing we saw before turning onto the highway, leaving the whole town to shrink smaller and smaller until it was a sleepy looking hamlet in the valley below.

We rode toward the rising sun and I felt brand new. We were leaving behind a town that had confined us in its narrow definitions, off to write our own stories in a city that promised endless possibilities and new beginnings.

DEAR RICKY

Dear Ricky,

I hope this letter finds you well. By the time you read it, I'll probably be well on my way to New York City, chasing dreams and not letting a good thing die when it's starting to grow. I wanted to tell you in person, but I knew you'd try to talk me out of it, and this is something I have to do.

First things first, I'm leaving Stilson's to you. I'm signing over the whole business so it's yours. You've been there for me through thick and thin, always reliable, always giving me the time. You're one of a kind, Ricky. Salt of the Earth. You've been more than a friend; you've been like a brother to me. I'll never forget our late-night antics, the laughs, the hard times we got through together, detention, suspension and all the crazy things. You've got a way of making the unbearable seem irrelevant, and I'm going to miss that. I'm going to miss you.

I know you might be wondering why I'm suddenly leaving, especially on such short notice. The truth is, I've been stuck in a loop here, like an old record that keeps skipping. I've been given a chance to break free, and I'm taking it. You're right, I won't let Morgan get away. I can't let this thing that started to grow between us die. I'm sick of all the death. I'm sure I can get on my feet there. It's risky, but it's a risk I have to take.

I want you to know that this isn't goodbye, not really. It's just a 'see you later.' I'll be back to visit, and you better have a cold one waiting for me when I do come back to town.

And so, my friend, I leave you with this: once you tune into the vibe of living, the adventure called life becomes a song you can't stop humming, a rhythm you can't stop moving to. It's a journey with no final destination, only endless horizons.

Take care, Ricky. Keep the vibe alive.

Your friend always,
Pete

THE MORE THINGS
CHANGE

T he weight of the memories pressed on me as I sat in my car, still unable to go the rest of the way. I had come back to Snydersville for Troy's funeral. A day I had always dreaded, a day I knew deep down would eventually come. In the thirty years since that trying time, the situation up here got worse, not better. The ways to hurt yourself got more plentiful, not less available.

I exhaled, shifted the gear into drive and drove down the roadway until I merged onto the exit ramp, the county road stretching before me like a timeline of my past.

Snydersville had been ravaged by the years, a victim of global shifts and local apathy as the economy grew worse for the rust belt. Troy had been a casualty too, his life a series of employment and unemployment periods until another back injury left him permanently disabled this time and then came the prescription for Percocet, "perks" as he called them. I'd get voice mails that asked for money, for help. I sent some, cautiously, always fearing I was enabling his darker habits. When he got his workman's comp settlement, my worst fears came true. He spiraled and started using crystal meth, and in the end, he was found alone, dead on the same old couch, a victim of his own vices and a world always ready to turn the grip a little harder on the Troy McCloskey types. The anger I felt dissolved into an overwhelming sadness as I drove into town.

I had distanced myself from Snydersville for a reason—it was a well of personal pain and depression, even though I had managed to escape its gravitational pull. Now in my late 40s, I took in the haunting beauty of the rolling hills that framed the valley. It was as if the land itself was painting a tragic portrait about its inhabitants, a narrative of pain, loss, and the rugged resilience of its people, because not all who remained here have fallen into hard times. The concrete jungle of NYC made people softer. This region of Western New York could not be survived without being a little hard.

Stilson's Liquor Store had transformed into Larson's Lounge, a full-fledged bar and restaurant that does quite well from what I have read on Ricky's Facebook page. I decided to stop in before heading to the funeral parlor, curious to see what Ricky had accomplished with the place. We lost touch long ago, simply grew apart in every way, but thanks to social media I was able to keep up with some of the good things that happened in his life.

The moment I stepped inside, nostalgia washed over me. The space had been upgraded; tables and chairs now occupied the spots where liquor and wine racks once stood. The cooler wall had been replaced by a long, wooden bar. A young waitress, no more than 17, approached me.

"I'm sorry. We're closed today for a private party today," she informed me.

"I know. I'll be there. I wanted to see what Ricky's done with the place," I replied. Her expression changed. "You're Pete McCloskey."

"That's me. Ricky and I go way back."

"He talks about you all the time. You're a legend here." She pointed to a framed letter hanging above a booth in the corner. "That's your letter to Ricky."

I walked over and stared at the framed letter, a tangible relic of my memories. "That's incredible," I said, knowing now how small acts can have a profound impact on someone's life. Giving Ricky the store had changed his trajectory, and that thought made me happy.

"Well, I should head to the funeral. I'll see you afterward," I told her.

"Nice meeting you, Mr. McCloskey," she said.

I chuckled as I walked out the door. "Mr. McCloskey." It sounded so formal, so distant. I was an artist, a simple man still trying to reconcile his past with his present.

I got back into my car and drove toward the funeral home, ready to close out the Snydersville chapter for good. Life, I've come to realize, is a tapestry of interconnected stories. We're all characters in a grand narrative, and while parents often dominate the early chapters, they're not the entire book. They have their own tales to tell, their own arcs to complete. It's a realization that's served me well, especially given my unlikely career as an author and screenwriter. The essence of any story lies in its structure: a beginning, a middle, and an end. How we fill the pages of each chapter is entirely up to us. Sometimes, you have to be taught how to take the pen into your own hands and write your own ending, even if it means diverging from the path laid out for you. And that's what I did.

The funeral home was tucked away on a side street, nestled at the base of the hill that had once been my world. I couldn't see our old house from here, but glancing in its direction, beyond the riverbank, gave a sense of bittersweet nostalgia. That hill was a repository of pain, but now, it all felt like passages from an old book I'd read long ago. I took a deep breath, letting the air fill my lungs before exhaling slowly, as if releasing the ghosts of my past once and for all.

I made my way toward the entrance. That's when I saw him—Little T., approaching from the opposite direction. Age had caught up with him; he was heavier now and leaned on a cane for support. But beyond those physical changes, the essence of Little T. remained unchanged. His eyes still held that same spark, that same lighthearted way that had always defined him.

As we neared each other, our eyes met, and for a moment, time stood still. Here we were, two characters from the same story, each having navigated our own set of trials and tribulations, converging once again at a pivotal moment together. It was a reminder that while chapters may close, the story continues, shaped by the choices we make and the people who enter our lives, even if only for a brief time.

As Little T. and I closed the distance between us, he looked at me with a mix of sorrow and understanding. "Pete, man, I'm so sorry about Troy, he loved you, man," he said.

"Thanks, LT," I replied, my voice catching slightly. "It means a lot to hear that from you."

He nodded, and for a moment, we stood there, two old friends sharing an unspoken bond. Then, breaking the silence, we moved in for a bro hug, a simple gesture of support.

As we pulled away, the door to the funeral home swung open, and Ricky's voice rang out, filling the air with a sense of familiarity that was both comforting and surreal. "If you're tardy, you'll be getting some in-school suspension!" he called out, a playful grin stretching across his face.

I found myself laughing—a genuine, heartfelt laugh that I hadn't realized I so desperately needed. "Ricky, you haven't changed one bit," I said, still chuckling as Little T. and I made our way toward the entrance.

Once inside, Ricky and I locked eyes, and without a word, we embraced. "I missed you, brother," he said. "Thank you for everything, Pete."

"I missed you too, Ricky," I replied, feeling completeness here, amidst the sorrow and the memories, surrounded by the people who had shaped my past, reminding me that we never truly leave behind the places—or the people—that make us who we are.

Ricky had taken it upon himself to arrange Troy's funeral, a gesture that didn't surprise me. Ricky was the kind of guy who would give you the shirt off his back if you needed it. He had always kept an eye on Troy, especially after hard drugs hit the town in the past few years, leaving a trail of devastation in their wake. It's a harsh reality that you can't save someone who doesn't want to be saved.

I entered the dimly lit room and saw a smattering of faces—people who had known Troy in various capacities, mostly his drinking buddies and a few old classmates who had never left Snydersville. They were seated in short rows, their expressions a mix of sadness and resignation.

I made my way to the memory table, where a collection of photographs had been arranged. They were snapshots of Troy's life—some from better days, others that painfully captured the toll that years of struggle had taken on him. In the center of the table was a silver tin adorned with the railroad logo, a final nod to Troy's intermittent career and dreams. It held his ashes.

Seeing that tin, something inside me broke. I hadn't prepared myself for the visceral impact of that moment—the finality of it all, the realization that Troy was truly gone and reduced to this. My eyes blurred, I muttered apologies, as if saying "I'm so sorry" over and over could somehow make up for all the years I wasn't there, for all the help I couldn't give, for not saving him from himself when he needed it most.

"I'm so sorry, Troy. I'm so, so sorry," I choked out, my voice barely above a whisper but heavy with regret.

I felt a gentle hand on my shoulder. It was the priest. "It's time to take your seat," he said softly.

Nodding, I wiped away my tears and took a deep, steadying breath. As I turned away from the table and walked toward an empty chair, I couldn't shake the feeling that this was more than a farewell to Troy. It was a confrontation with my own guilt, my own missed opportunities, and the haunting question of whether I could have changed the course of his tragic story had I stuck around. And as I sat down, I knew that this was a chapter in my life that would never truly be closed.

The reception at Larson's Lounge was the kind of medicine my soul needed. The place was filled with familiar faces, some aged by time and hardship, others surprisingly unchanged as if nothing happened in all these years. Ricky had done an incredible job. It was a testament to his resilience and good nature, qualities that had always defined him. Larson's Lounge had become a local hot spot that everyone went to.

As I made my way through the crowd, nursing a drink and sharing stories with old friends, I felt a tap on my shoulder. I turned around and was met with a face I never thought I'd be happy to see—Chad Parks. But something was different about him. The menacing glare that used to frame his beady eyes was replaced by a warm, genuine smile. He was thinner, smaller, wearing stylish clothes and had an air about him that I knew well now. Standing beside him was a man I didn't recognize, but who exuded the same kind-hearted energy.

"Chad?" I said, putting my hand forward to shake his. "Wow."

"It's really good to see you, Pete. I'm sorry about Troy, oh and this is Kevin, my husband," Chad introduced us, his voice softer and more mature than I remembered. "I'm so sorry about your brother," said Kevin.

"Thanks. Nice to meet you, Kevin," I said, extending my hand to him as well, still somewhat in disbelief at Chad's transformation.

"Likewise," Kevin replied. "I've heard a lot about you. I can't believe what a super meany pants my man was back in the day."

"Ah well. We were dumb and young. It's all good. What do you do these days, Chad?"

"We own a business together in Rochester. Refurbishing old furniture and selling it. It's been a dream come true."

"That's amazing. I'm really happy for you," I said, genuinely pleased to hear about his new life but still baffled that he was gay all along.

Chad looked a bit hesitant before speaking again, "Look, Pete, I came down here not only to pay my respects, but to find you and apologize. I really was a mega jerk back in the day, and I'm sorry for all the times I made your life miserable."

I looked into his eyes and saw sincerity, a far cry from the tormentor of my youth. "No worries, man."

Chad laughed nervously, "Turns out, I thought you were cute and didn't like that part of myself back then."

We laughed and I couldn't help but smile at the irony. "I'm glad you found your true self. And I'm glad you found happiness with Kevin."

Chad's eyes softened, "Thanks, Pete. That means a lot."

As we parted, I was reminded that people could change, that past wrongs could be made right, and that sometimes, the most unexpected reunions could be the most healing. As I mingled with Ricky, Little T., and other townsfolk I hadn't seen in years, a recurring question kept surfacing.

"Why didn't Morgan come home with you?"

The inquiry was tinged with a bit of longing for the girl who had once been a beacon of hope in this struggling town. Her success was no secret around here and neither was our marriage. Her mom passed a few years back and we both hadn't been around since.

"She's in surgery today, operating on a very young patient who needs the world's best and that's Morgan McCloskey," I explained. "She really wanted to be here, but when you're in the business of saving lives, you can't walk away."

The nods that followed were understanding, respectful. "You must be so proud of her," someone said, capturing the sentiment of the room.

"Proud doesn't even begin to describe it," I replied, my eyes momentarily distant as I thought of her. "The word 'proud' feels almost inadequate when I think about how much I love Morgan."

"Cheers to that," said Ricky and we clinked glasses and drank.

In that moment, despite the weight of these tragic events, I felt a sense of gratitude for the journey that had led me here, for the chapters yet to be written, and for the people who had become the indelible characters in the story of my life.

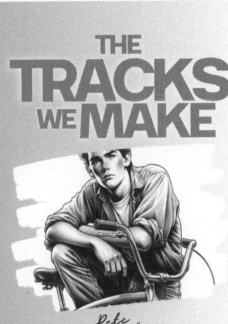

THE
TRACKS
WE MAKE

Pete McCloskey

About the Author

Michael McGruther is a storyteller who left a small town for the bustle of New York City. His journey started in 1991, first as an actor booking small parts in feature films (Clockers, In & Out), national TV commercials, radio ads, and a star turn in Nickelodeon's "The Swirlies" TV pilot.

Michael's true calling was to tell stories. He co-wrote "Tigerland," which launched an international star, and continued to pen screenplays for Hollywood studios and independent producers before diving into the realm of indie publishing. His debut, "The Puddle Club," garnered the Kirkus Star and was hailed as one of the best new indies of 2018.

Converting old screenplay ideas into novels with "Crisis Moon" and "OMIM," Michael's sci-fi books are fast-paced portals to futures both thrilling and thought-provoking.

His latest, "SubPopCult - The New Reiteration," is a manifesto that converges the threads of culture, storytelling, and policy — themes that he focuses on in his celebrated podcast.